A CHILD
OF
COLOGNE

David Maybe

Dedication

*To all who help to provide
sanctuary.*

Preface

The story that follows may be described as an historical novel, but this feels strange as it takes place largely in my lifetime. It contains both historical and fictional characters. Any resemblance between the fictional ones and persons, living or dead (except myself) is purely coincidental.

I would like to take this opportunity to thank the members of the Old Hall Community in East Bergholt, (birthplace of John Constable), for their friendship over many years. Also, Catherine Fitzsimons, my editor, for all the very helpful advice she has given me. Peter of Bespoke Book Covers for my beautiful and imaginative book cover and Lorna Lee for making the publication of my book possible.

Above all, I want to thank my wife Janet for all her loving care, including the invaluable input she has made to this book.

If you have enjoyed reading or listening to this story you may wish to consider sending a donation to:

The Refugee Council,
PO Box 68614
London E15 9DQ

David Maybe
September 2018

Prologue

"Oh God! Where's Mummy?" Olga stumbled. The menacing mists of November chilled her. Out of the gloom she could hear, again and again, the shattering of glass. The journey home from school was usually a time of joyful expectancy. She would look forward to her grandmother opening the door and releasing the smell of freshly baked bread. Often they would dance together up and down the steps of their home.

There was no joy today. Mother was missing and she had that letter. The one that had appeared in her satchel.

> *Dear Olga,*
> *Your life is in danger. Please escape from Cologne as soon as possible.*
> *May God bless and protect you.*
> *A friend of Agamemnon*

Olga had almost reached the haven of Wilhelmstrasse when she heard a bell ringing. The sound came closer and closer. Then a swastika-decorated fire engine passed her. It turned the corner. Olga ran. She ran even faster than she had from the Herman twins. She could see smoke billowing from her home. She reached it just as a stretcher was being brought out. Before she lifted the blanket, she knew her grandmother lay under it.

The body was black.

That was the problem; her grandmother had always been black.

PART ONE

Germany

A Child of Cologne

1

Olga Leaves her Sanctuary

19 May 1922

Olga had struggled hard and long to escape from the cave but now, when she was at last free, she was completely bewildered. She was overwhelmed by unfamiliar sights and sounds, smells and feelings. There were no words to describe the utterly strange experiences she was encountering. Fortunately, the outside of the cave was soft and warm and comforting. Nevertheless, she couldn't help feeling that she had just made the biggest mistake of her life. She wondered whether she would ever feel as safe and secure again as she had felt for so long in the cave.

That was when she started to scream.

Gradually, she became aware of a gentle background murmur and a steady, familiar rhythm.

That was when she stopped screaming.

Several hours later Olga heard louder noises. She had heard them before, from time to time, but now they were much clearer and nearer. Whether they were important or not she neither knew nor cared. All that mattered was that she still had the comfort of her rock and the sweet nourishment that flowed from it. Then the rock's centre of attention seemed to move from her to the source of the new noise. Terrified of losing everything, Olga began screaming again. She did she not know that the noises were coming from her adoring parents, Ursula and Heinrich.

2

Ursula

Ursula put her arms around Olga who stopped screaming.

Heinrich put his arms around them both and kept saying, "Thank you. Thank you for our lovely daughter. Thank you for Olga," and variants on that theme, kissing his wife and daughter each time. Suddenly, he stopped and reached behind himself to pick up a large bunch of yellow roses.

"My favourite flowers! I've never seen such a large bouquet. How many are there?"

"There are a dozen from me, my love, and seven from my mother. She sends her love and says that each of her roses is for one of your seven virtues. She'll visit you tomorrow; she can't wait to see her granddaughter and, of course, you."

"Please give her my thanks and my love. Oh! I love you so much! I'm so grateful for all your thoughtful care."

Heinrich smiled and said, "I remember the moment I first saw you."

Ursula knew exactly what he was going to say next but luxuriated in anticipation.

"It was eleven minutes past eleven on the eleventh day of the eleventh month of 1913. The first minute of the carnival. I looked across the road and saw a vision with hair, shoes and socks the colour of these roses, eyes the colour of bluebells, a skirt to match and a white blouse which fitted your lovely body beautifully. I tried to cross the road to reach you, to speak to you but the crowd surged forward and I lost sight of you. I searched miserably for hours but, in the end, I had to give up hope. I thought that I'd lost you for ever so I went home and painted a picture of you from memory."

At this point in his reverie he was brought back to the present by someone shouting, "Herr Muller! Visiting time was over ten minutes ago. You may think you're above the law, but your friend Adenauer isn't here to look after you today. Just as well, or he'd get a mouthful from me. Never once during the

8

war did he come here to visit the men who had been wounded protecting him – and the rest of us. You wait until the workers are in power. We know how to deal with scum like him and subhumans like you. We nearly got there in 1918 but our so-called leaders betrayed us. Next time there will be a real leader, one worthy of the German people."

Heinrich opened his mouth to reply but was silenced by Ursula putting her finger to her lips. "You'd better go, my love, or Nurse Tyrann will report us to Sister."

Sadly, Ursula watched Heinrich go and then she fed Olga. She lay down with her baby (her baby!) in her arms, but sleep would not come. Memory after memory came flooding back.

She remembered her childhood, growing up beside the Rhine amongst the vineyards of Rhöndorf and climbing up through the Siebengebirge to the Schloss Drachenburg to absorb the breath -taking view below. She remembered her first and only visit to the carnival's opening ceremony and that rather handsome boy who had stared at her for so long. She remembered the middle of the war, and being a nurse herself in this very hospital.

***

One day, at the beginning of her morning shift, a member of the departing night shift had come threateningly close to her and hissed, "There's a new patient in bed four. He's mine! I saw him first. Simpering, pretty nurses like you seem to think you can have any man you want, but not this time. If you dare encourage him at all, I'll make your life not worth living!" And then she had marched smartly away.

Ursula wondered what that was about. Relationships with the soldiers were not permitted and, anyway, the idea would never have occurred to her. During her training, the nuns who ran the hospital, had made clear that a nurse's task was to make the men physically better while reminding them that they were valued children of God. The nurses must certainly not remind their patients that they were men – helpless men, maybe, but still men. The nurses were girls and, therefore, according to the nuns, vulnerable.

Ursula went straight to the dying man in bed one. She stayed with him, providing small words of comfort, until a priest arrived to offer him extreme unction. As she watched his young life disappear, she wanted to scream against the senseless waste – but she managed to keep her treasonable thoughts to herself. Bed two contained a man blinded by tear gas and in three was one who had lost his right arm. She had done her best for each of them but knew that all the hospital could provide was palliative care.

She had approached bed four deep in thought, but then stopped a few steps short of it when she recognised the face. She had seen it many times in her dreams; it was the face of the boy at the carnival. His eyes were closed. When he opened them, he spoke to her in a deep, soft voice. Ursula couldn't recognise the accent. He was certainly not using Kolnish or any other Rhineland dialect, and he didn't sound Prussian or Bavarian but more like an actor in a play by Schiller.

"Please come closer," he began. But he stumbled over the next word, hesitated, and said 'angel' instead of 'nurse'. She came forward and he continued, "There's a wallet in the top pocket of my jacket. Please take it out and open it."

When Ursula opened it, she thought she saw herself in a mirror. But the mirror was odd: it was not made of glass, the reflection

11

did not move when she did and she looked five years younger. Mesmerised, she heard the faint voice of the man in the bed.

"I painted this picture as soon as I got home and I've kept it on me ever since."

***

The tired new mother drifted off to sleep, dreamily thinking about her wedding day.

On the first night of their honeymoon, Heinrich had undressed her gently but firmly. She revelled in the delight she felt each time he expressed wonder at a freshly revealed part of her beauty. She was very happy to see from his reactions that he was a virgin – despite his time in the army. Heinrich had lifted her up and tenderly placed her on their bed.

***

When Heinrich had proposed to her she had accepted with a bright smile on her face. However, behind the façade she was concerned that the pain of his injury might mean his chances of being able to consummate their union were no more than fifty-fifty. She was anxious to improve the odds, but kept her fears to herself because she did not want to damage his self-confidence. In the end she had decided there was only one thing to do and, in the weeks before the wedding, she kept a sharp eye open for an opportunity.

It came on 16 August, two days before the wedding and, therefore, two days before she would have to leave her employment. A colleague was careless, giving her the chance to pounce on some strong painkilling drugs. As soon as she had got them, a great wave of fear flowed through her body; should she be caught, she would end up in prison.

The next day, she confessed to Father Mathias, the hospital chaplain.

"Stealing is a sin, whatever your motives. But I can't help thinking that, in these circumstances, Our Lord would forgive you. However, I'm worried about the danger of Heinrich receiving a fatal dose."

She reassured him, saying, "I'm a highly experienced nurse and you can be sure I'll be extra careful!"

He nodded, "I understand your honeymoon will be in Rhöndorf. I'll be there in a week's time so that the parish priest can have a holiday. Should you wish to visit me

at the presbytery, I would be very pleased to
see you both."

3

Heinrich

WHen Heinrich got back to their flat he poured himself a large glass of sherry. He did not drink much but, on this occasion, said to himself, "I deserve this." He went to bed but could not sleep. He just lay there thinking about the baby he and Ursula had managed to produce, and about how much he loved them both. He remembered how Ursula had helped him with his persistent nightmares, the scenes that had run through his head like a film. She had begged him to reveal what caused him such terror. When he could no longer resist her pleas, he had told her.

***

"Each night when I fall asleep the same face appears in my dreams," he said. "I'm back in those dreadful trenches and the lines of British Tommies are bearing down on us with fixed bayonets. I hear the order to fire

15

and obey, but don't know whether I've hit anyone. All I know is that they're continuing to advance. I recharge my rifle and fire at the nearest Tommy, who's right in front of me. He falls into the trench and his bayonet pierces my leg. The pain is terrible and his weight thrusting it down makes it worse. His body is lying on top of me so I can hardly move. We lie pinned together for what seems like ages. He mutters a lot – but in English so, of course, I don't understand him. And then, with his dying breath, he says '*Mater Dei.*' And then the stretcher bearers arrive and carry him off to his grave and me to hospital."

"And it is the face of that Catholic British soldier you see in your dreams." Heinrich nodded. There was no need for more words at this stage. Ursula could understand his reasons for feeling troubled without them being spelt out. She lay on the bed, cradling Heinrich in her arms for a while before saying, "I happen to know that Father Mathias is visiting Rhöndorf today and is staying at the presbytery overnight. I think that now would be a good time to visit him."

The couple got dressed and walked together down the hill.

The priest admitted them and said to Heinrich, "I was about to have a beer; will you join me?" Heinrich nodded and Ursula said.

"You don't mind if I go and help Father with the drinks and tell him about your nightmares, do you?" Without waiting for an answer, she followed the priest into the kitchen and closed the door behind them. After a while, she emerged and said, "Father will hear your confession now."

In a daze, Heinrich went into the other room. After a period of silence and the usual preliminaries, Father Mathias asked him to repeat what he had told Ursula. Hesitantly, and with great difficulty, he did so. A much longer period of silence followed. Heinrich waited in dread for the judgement of his confessor. Finally, the priest raised his head, took the young man's hands into his own and told him to say one *Hail Mary* for the soul of the dead man. Heinrich could not believe his ears until he heard the addendum. "And you are to do this every day for the rest of your life."

Father Mathias led the way back into the other room where Ursula was waiting for her husband with an extra-special pint of beer.

Heinrich noticed something different about the taste, but was too polite to say anything.

In silent contemplation, the lovers walked hand in hand back to their hotel and their bed. Heinrich had little trouble overcoming the problem that had prevented full marital union until then.

Olga was conceived that very night.

***

The next morning, Ursula felt that she should tell her husband what she had done, although she was fearful of his response. But Heinrich said, "What a clever, brave and thoughtful wife I've got! I love you so much! I just wish that I could show my love in the way a husband should."

Ursula was quiet for a moment, and then replied, "I think that we'll find many ways of showing our love for each other over the coming years."

And they did.

The Tommy never again haunted the dreams of the man who had killed him. Instead, Heinrich sensed forgiveness enveloping him each day as he prayed for the repose of the soul of the soldier towards whom he gradually developed a feeling of camaraderie.

Before leaving Rhöndorf, the couple visited Father Mathias again to thank him for his help and bring him up to date. The priest took the opportunity to ask Heinrich what he thought of his new boss, Herthe Krause.

"I have a high regard for Herr Adenauer, but I can't understand why he has appointed a woman. Especially as she doesn't come from Cologne. She isn't even a Catholic," Heinrich said.

"I too have a very high regard for our mayor, and will always be grateful for the way he managed to keep the city running and its people fed during the war – and ever since," said Father Mathias. "I understand Fraulein Krause is highly qualified. It is a pity she's not a Catholic, but she is a Quaker and you'll be well aware of how much work that sect is doing to help Germany, Cologne in particular."

Ursula noted silently that he made no comment about Herthe Krause's gender.

A Child of Cologne

4

The Christening

URsula and Olga left the hospital and joined Heinrich in the home he shared with his mother, Sophia. The adults had hoped to have the christening in the cathedral and were delighted when the canon agreed. It was not only a wonderful setting for the sacred ceremony but also a place of special memories for Heinrich.

Soon afterwards Ursula's mother came to visit from the family's new home near Bonn. Ursula loved her mother, and greatly admired her ability to manipulate her patrician husband. It was she who had persuaded him to reluctantly drop his resistance to the marriage. She had been less successful with Otto and Marguerite, Ursula's older siblings, but they had known better than to continue to protest after their father had capitulated. Frau Nachtigall was alone. Her husband and older children had clearly boycotted the visit but, instead of explaining their absence, she announced that Marguerite and Otto were to be the child's godparents. Only a look from Ursula prevented Heinrich from shouting an obscenity he rarely used.

"I presume those are Father's wishes," Ursula sighed. "I can't think of anyone less suitable. I expect he thinks that having them stand amongst such illustrious figures as the archbishop and the lord mayor will add to the family honour. You had to fight so hard to get him to accept my marriage in the first place that I feel I have no choice but to agree to this."

Her mother then dropped another bombshell. "He wants you and the baby to spend a few days with us before the ceremony and then for us – the mother, the baby, the godparents and their parents – to travel together from Bonn to the cathedral in Otto's new car."

"I am not travelling in Otto's new toy. And what about the other grandmother – let alone the baby's father?"

"Your father has agreed to let Olga's father and Frau Muller attend the service as long as they are not too conspicuous. And he won't budge about the car. He thinks it will raise Otto's prestige if other lawyers get to see it."

Ursula wearily decided that it was no good fighting further over the car. And she knew that the church authorities would see to it that her husband and his mother were treated with every courtesy.

***

On the morning of the christening, there was a frost. Otto woke late but, of course, that was not his fault – or so he shouted. He shouted more unrepeatable words when the car would not start. To listen to him, one would not think that it was the thing he most loved in the world. Otto did not dare to reply when his father rebuked him, pointing that they were in danger of being late. All the same, he reflected, all the shouting wasn't helping. Eventually, the engine spluttered into life and they were off. Otto knew what his car was capable of and he knew that they could make it on time – although, now, only just.

As they entered the suburbs of Cologne, his right eye caught a fast movement. He tried to take avoiding action, but he hit the dog that had run into the road. Although it was only a glancing blow, Otto stopped the car. Without thinking, Ursula put Olga into Marguerite's lap and climbed out. The dog was obviously badly injured but still alive. It had a nametag and its owner's name and address round its neck: *The Lindens*. Ursula looked up and saw that name outside the nearest house. She scooped the mongrel up in her arms, carried it to the front door and rang the bell. As soon as the door was answered, she hurriedly handed the animal over with a short apology, turned, and ran back to the car. Otto was cursing more than ever but now his venom was directed at his "stupid sister".

They arrived ten minutes late. Everyone was there: the archbishop in his robes, the lord mayor in his ceremonial garb, the canon, the priests and many well-wishers … but the two people Ursula looked for most keenly were her husband and his mother. When she found them, she realised they were staring at her, looking worried. She looked down at her new, very expensive, yellow dress. It was covered in dirt and blood! Before Ursula knew what was happening, Sophia came over. She took off the leopard-skin coat that had been her wedding present from her late husband and draped it round Ursula's shoulders, thus hiding the offending sight.

***

Three months later Ursula and Heinrich were at a very different christening. Ilse, the mother, had been Ursula's best friend at school. The absent father was a Moroccan soldier from the French army of occupation. He had raped Ilse. She would have liked her child to have a godparent from Rhöndorf, to be around to keep a close eye on his spiritual growth – but nobody in the village had wanted anything to do with her disgrace.

Ursula held the baby in her arms while the priest named him Balthazar. He went on to explain to the small congregation that, according to legend, this was the name of the African wise man who had visited Jesus at his birth and was now buried, with his two companions, at Cologne cathedral.

A Child of Cologne

5

Artist's Inspirations

Olga had a happy childhood. Her mother looked after her and the home. When Olga was unwell, which was not often, she was comforted by her mother's professional yet loving care. Grandma did the cooking and Olga enjoyed 'helping'. She did not enjoy helping her mother with the housework but recognised that was what girls did. Men, especially German men, went out to work to feed their families. At least, that was the theory. But even Olga's young mind was aware that it was not always the practice. She was sorry it was the practice in their family because she would very much have liked her father to be home more often. He was a calm, quiet man who spent much of his time smiling as if at a private joke and referred to his family as his 'three ladies'.

This year, Olga's mother had bought him a very exciting birthday present and Olga had been sworn to secrecy. She was not to tell him anything. Daddy was clever and guessed that there was a secret in the air but, although he quizzed her a number of times, she managed to keep her promise. There was never enough time at breakfast, so they waited until he came home from work. Olga begged her mother to be the one to hand the carefully wrapped parcel to her father. He opened it gently (Olga could not understand why he had not torn the paper off the way she always did). His eyes glowed with excitement and pleasure as he brought out lots and lots of artist's materials: oil paints and watercolours, a palette, brushes, paper, board and a painter's apron. He had been dabbling with painting for some time, creating pictures on scrap paper. "I know you're a good artist already, but I think you could be even better with the right materials," said Ursula. "That's why Olga and I have bought you these." Olga inwardly hugged herself with delight on hearing Mummy say the present was from her too! Her father hugged and kissed them both several times. Olga thought he kissed her mother more times than he kissed her – but who was counting! She felt very happy.

Then her grandmother said, "I have a present for Heinrich, too." And she produced, from where Olga could not fathom, an even larger parcel. When Heinrich opened it, Olga gasped and jumped up and down. It was a proper artist's easel. Heinrich was even more excited than his daughter, but it was not his practice to show his emotions. However, the two older women in his life knew him well enough to recognise the depth of his gratitude.

The next day was Saturday and in the morning he took Olga with him when he went to the cathedral with some of his materials.

"What are you going to paint first? The part of the altarpiece with Saint Ursula and the virgins in honour of Mummy?"

"No. I don't think she'd particularly want a picture of her name saint. What I think she – and you – would like is the scene from the nativity window. Especially the ox and the delightful braying donkey."

"Oh, that's a wonderful idea!"

Heinrich led his daughter through the Portal of Mary in the west façade. Not for the first time, he boasted that it was the largest façade of any church in the whole world and, not for the first time, she did not say that she was not interested. What she *was* interested in were the statues round the portal – but they were not coloured and her father ignored them. Once inside, she looked all the way down the nave to the far distant windows. The one at the bottom, beneath the window of the kings, was their target.

Olga loved this view. The windows were too far away to allow them to make out individual figures, but they radiated beautiful colours as they had done for over six hundred years. Yes, it was very large but it was also very beautiful and, although she was only small, she could take it in. The façade, she thought, was just very large. She had to crick her neck to look at that properly. She made her father stop while she looked at the shapes of the pillars, the soaring graceful vaulting, and the statues.

They walked slowly down the aisle, past the ornate shrine until, eventually, they reached the chapel of the magi. Heinrich hurried them through this part of the cathedral with barely concealed dislike. It was not the first time they had been there and it was not the first time she had sensed his unease. "Why don't you like that chapel, Daddy? It's where the wise men who came to visit the baby Jesus are buried."

"Oh! sorry! I didn't think you'd noticed!" He had not planned to tell her, but he explained anyway. "I don't believe that the Empress Helena found their tomb, but I could be wrong. What I am sure of is that it was wicked for our archbishop to support the emperor Barbarossa's war against his fellow Christians in Milan and to accept these relics as a reward. Many good men, on both sides, died terrible deaths in the battle."

Olga saw tears in her father's eyes and dried his eyes little knowing that he was crying for a particular Tommie rather than all those soldiers of long ago.

They sat down in front of the window and Olga watched for a while, quietly fascinated, as her father made several sketches. Much of the time, he just sat there absorbing what he saw and describing the exact shades of each part of the picture. There were shades of yellow and blue, grey for the ass and white for the swaddling clothes of the baby Jesus lying in the manger. He particularly noted the colours of the Virgin's clothing: the

31

convention was to paint her dressed in blue but, remembering what he had been told of Olga's birth, he thought the red the artist had chosen for her skirts was not inappropriate. The top of her robe was green – for rebirth, perhaps.

Olga had expected him to paint the window in a flash so, after a while, her fascination waned and she became restless. She 'borrowed' a pencil and a sheet of paper from her father's stack and wandered off. Although she had been to many services in the cathedral, she had never before been able to wander off and see things for herself. Everywhere she looked, there were fresh wonders and delights. It was an Aladdin's cave. It was impossible to pick one out to draw; that would mean rejecting all the others. Then, near the south entrance, she saw the figure of Saint Christopher and Olga was struck by the expression on his face. He was twice life size and carried a small Christ-child on his shoulder. But Jesus was holding the world in his hands and the weight was clearly almost too much for the saint to bear. Olga found a spot on the ground nearby to squat and copy the agony on his face. She then sketched in the rest of his body, his staff and the holy boy.

As she finished she heard a voice frantically shouting her name in the silence. Her father had been searching for her and hadn't been able to find her. They were late for lunch and his mother's cooking would be wasted. They hurried home and shamefacedly blurted out their apologies. But, when Sophia saw what they had done, she quickly forgave them and made a substitute meal.

That afternoon, Heinrich found his easel and started to convert his morning's work into a painting. Olga found her skipping rope and went into the garden to play. Heinrich was not satisfied with his painting and put it away – but his next attempt was much more successful. He kept learning from his mistakes and got better and better.

Olga again joined him for the morning and this time Ursula promised to come and find them in plenty of time for lunch. Olga did not feel the need to improve her earlier work and moved on to a new statue. "There are enough here to last you a lifetime!" warned her father. "As well as all the medieval statues, there are seven hundred created by Peter

Fuchs and his team in the nineteenth century."

***

Over the following months and years, Heinrich painted many pictures and his daughter sketched many statues but there was one subject they both avoided: the Gero Cross, a larger-than-life-size oak cross bearing the body of Christ at the moment of his death, the moment mankind was redeemed. Heinrich knew with all his being that his gift was not great enough to do adequate honour to the suffering on the face of the man on this cross. Subconsciously, Olga felt the same and knew instinctively that it would not be right for her to attempt to make an image of this thousand-year-old icon.

6
The Earthquake

T hrough the 1920s, the Muller adults were concerned by the increasing numbers of brownshirts marching along the streets of Cologne. And their concern increased when the Nazis were attacked by gangs of Marxists. From time to time, Heinrich would come home from the city hall with an exciting rumour – Herr Adenauer was about to be made chancellor of Germany – but the rumours never solidified into fact. Some other leader from the Centre Party was always chosen instead.

Near the end of the decade, Heinrich reported to his family that the mayor had spoken to the staff about how the city had prospered since the war, thanks in no small measure to the hard work they had put in. However, he'd also made clear that the events taking place in Wall Street would have severe effects, even in Germany, and they needed to prepare and make plans to mitigate the damage. What the mayor had not foreseen was the astounding rise of the Nazi Party. The Mullers watched in impotent horror as, in election after election, the people they feared increased their share of the vote, going up from 3% in 1928 to 37% in 1932.

But then the rumbles gave way to the earthquake itself: on 31 January 1933 Adolf Hitler was appointed as chancellor.

Shortly after that, Heinrich came home with the news that he and his colleagues had all been dismissed. Herr Adenauer was moving to another part of Germany, and Fraulein Kraus to a Quaker College in Pennsylvania. He announced to Ursula and Sophia that he would support them by selling his pictures to tourists.

"Thank you, darling, for being so brave," said Ursula. "But it's whistling in the dark. I think that, really, you know as well as I do that the income you'll be able to make from the sales will only scratch the surface. I've come to a decision: I'm going back to nursing."

"But you won't be allowed to. You're a married woman," protested Heinrich.

Ursula parried, saying, "I won't go back as a married woman but as Nurse Nachtigall. To do that, I'll need to move. Somewhere away from Cologne where people don't know of about you. I'm sorry, my love, but this is too important for us to take any risks."

There was silence in the room until her mother-in-law said, "Bless you, Ursula. Doing that takes great courage, thoughtfulness and love. The idea of being separated from you grieves me, but I think your solution is the only viable one."

Three weeks later, Ursula told Heinrich and Sophia that she'd obtained a post at Rhöndorf hospital. "Of course I'll thank Ilse for telling me about it, but I'll have to tell her that I can't risk going to see her. Visiting the mother of a Rhineland bastard will raise too many questions. I feel I'm betraying a friend who needs and deserves my support, but I've no choice. Will you please see Bal continues to get presents and cards?"

When Olga came home from school that day, Ursula picked the ten-year-old up, put her on her knee and said, "You know Daddy has lost his job?"

"Yes, but he's selling his pictures instead."

"That won't bring in enough for us to live on. So I'm going to be a nurse again. Unfortunately, I can't do that in Cologne so I'm going to the hospital in Rhöndorf."

"But … but … that's a long way away!"

"Yes, but I'll come home as often as I can. And I'll write to you every week."

By now, both Olga and Ursula were crying. They hugged each other for comfort and, after a while, Olga said, "I'll miss you so much! But I do feel very lucky that I'll still have Daddy and Grandma at home to care for me."

***

When Heinrich sent his first parcel to Bal it was returned. On it was a scribbled message:

Not known at this address.

7

The Neighbours

H ans Smit could not believe his eyes. He looked again from the bedroom window of his new home into the neighbours' courtyard. Yes! It was true. There was an African next door. She was hanging out washing and had her back to him but he had no doubt.

I've never seen an African, he thought. But I've seen pictures of them in school books and there is no question that she's African. The colour of her skin and the crinkliness of her hair are sure giveaways. A lot of people say that they are not properly human but the priests teach us that they are all God's children. I don't know what to think. Just then the woman turned, saw his face at the window and gave him a broad, radiant smile. Hans saw a well-built but graceful lady whose greying hair told him that she was old enough to be a grandmother. He watched her pick up the empty clothes basket and move back inside. For some moments he stood there stunned by this inter-continental encounter. I can't wait to get to school and tell Fritz; he won't believe me, he thought. Then it all came back to him. There was no more Fritz. No more Helmut, no more Wilhelm, no more Karl, no more Sister Magdalene. No more Saint Peter's – it had not been such a bad school after all. Most of all, however, no more Berlin. Hans had felt proud to be part of the greatest city of the greatest nation in the world. OK, he knew Germany had lots of problems at the moment, but his father kept on saying that things would get better soon, and Hans himself often sang Tomorrow Belongs to Me.

Remembering his father made him cross. "Why has Father brought us to this stupid, provincial city?" he wondered aloud. "Even the name reminds me of sissy girls."

He mimicked his father's deep voice. "Because I have been promoted!" But the sound turned sour in his mouth. Too readily, it reminded Hans of what had happened yesterday, on the first day at his new school.

A Child of Cologne

The teacher had introduced him to the other boys and asked him to say where he came from. Why he not been prepared for such an obvious question he did not know. All he knew was that his cheeks were red-hot with embarrassment as he stuttered, "*Ich bin ein Berliner, Mein Herr.*" Why on earth had he not said the more natural, "*Ich komme aus Berlin*"? But it was too late now. Throughout the breaks and lunchtime that day his new classmates had marched around him, stuttering "*Ich bin ein Berliner,*" in poor imitations of his Prussian accent. He had desperately wanted to cry but knew that, whatever else he did in his life, he could not and must not cry just then.

His reverie was interrupted. The door that the African lady had just shut reopened. This time a girl of about his own age came out with a skipping rope. Frieda, his little sister, often skipped and so Hans was not interested enough to watch. He turned away from the window and then turned back, thinking there was something different about the girl. He tried to work out what it was, but was left puzzled.

After breakfast, the new boy set off for Saint Boniface school – worrying about the

41

day ahead – while Frieda headed in the opposite direction, to the convent school. But the expected failed to happen. The boys' taunts had not got the reaction they wanted and so they had become bored with the game. At first he felt relieved that they were leaving him alone but, as the day wore on, he felt sadder and sadder. He was homesick and lonely but knew he should not be. His new home and his family were only just up the road. Nevertheless, he desperately missed Berlin and his friends and there was nothing he could do about it.

At the end of the school day, Hans walked home slowly, deep in thought. As he neared home he was startled to see Frieda walking hand in hand with the skipping rope girl. They arrived first and waited for him.

"This is Olga Muller who lives next door to us. She has asked me in to taste some of her grandma's apple strudel."

"And you're very welcome to come in, too," Olga added.

Lust for apple strudel – and curiosity – overcame his shyness and he went in with them. The elderly lady he had seen from the window offered him a tray of freshly baked strudels.

"My grandmother made them herself," Olga said proudly.

He took one. It not only smelt but also tasted delicious. After thoroughly enjoying the treat Hans remembered his manners and asked Olga where her grandmother was so he could thank her. There was a silence in the room and then the African lady stepped forward and hugged Hans.

"That's a very understandable mistake to make. A lot of other people have done the same. I'm Olga's grandmother; her father's mother."

Hans wished the floor would open up and swallow him but, after a moment, his mistake was forgotten as the four of them set to jabbering at each other.

"How are you enjoying Cologne?" Olga's grandmother asked Hans after a while. There was an uncomfortable silence. At last, he blurted out how much he missed his old school friends and mentioned Fritz in particular.

"Why don't you write a letter to him? I'm sure he'd like to get one and would write back with all his news. It won't be the same, but I think it will help. I found it a great help getting letters from my parents and friends

43

when I first came to Germany. Of course, letters took weeks to travel from Africa in those days but now, with airmail, I get letters from my friends and cousins in two or three days. Sadly, I no longer get letters from my parents because they both died a few years ago." Hans thought this was a great idea and decided that he would write the next day.

When they had eaten their strudel and drunk some lemonade, Olga's grandmother said to her, "Why don't you show Frieda and Hans your room?" She knew there was something Olga would be dying to show them, but that she and her parents were not supposed to know about it. Sophia tidied Olga's room regularly and was amused at the child's naivety. Nevertheless, she had not revealed her granddaughter's secret.

Olga led the way feeling very happy that she could, at last, share her secret. It was possible her parents and grandmother would understand but if neighbours found out it would bring great shame on the family – and they had enough problems without that. As they went upstairs, Hans discreetly took a handkerchief from his pocket and gently wiped the crumbs from around Frieda's lips.

When the children got to the bedroom, Olga put her finger to her lips and the others crept in behind her. She knelt down and lifted the eiderdown that hung down over the side of her bed. Hans was fascinated to see a baby rat nibbling on a piece of bread. Frieda screamed.

Downstairs, Sophia heard the scream and smiled quietly.

Olga put her hand over the younger girl's mouth and whispered, "It won't hurt you. It's only a baby and, in any case, rats only attack people if they are cornered and very frightened."

"Sorry, Olga," she said. But the rat had fled back into his hole.

Hans was very cross with his sister, but Frieda tried to make up for her fright by asking, "Is it a boy or a girl?"

"It's a boy."

"How do you know?"

Olga blushed. How could she explain in front of Hans? Perhaps she would find another opportunity to explain the facts of life to Frieda. For now, she limited her reply to, "I just know." However, inwardly, she gave thanks that her mother was a nurse who did not hesitate to talk to her about such matters. Ursula had told her that, even in this modern age, most mothers were too embarrassed to talk to their children about sex – sometimes until it was too late.

Hans interrupted her thoughts, asking if she had given the rat a name.

"No. I should have, shouldn't I? What do you suggest?"

Hans thought for a moment and then suggested Agamemnon.

"Why? I've never heard of him. Who was he?"

"He was the leader of the Greek armies who conquered Troy."

"That's a very grand name for a very small rat! But I like the sound of it. Yes. Let's call him Agamemnon." Olga suggested that they both came back after school the next day and she would introduce them to her little rodent friend properly.

***

The next day, Sophia gave each of them a scrumptious chocolate éclair. Hans was very pleased he had had the foresight to bring a rag with which to wipe Frieda's mouth – chocolate on his handkerchief would have looked awful. Agamemnon was on Olga's bed when they went, quietly, into her room. She sat on the bed and opened her clenched hand to reveal a bit of a honey sandwich. Hans stood, fascinated, while the creature sat on her hand and nibbled at the food. He had never been so close to a wild animal. When the rat had eaten as much as he wanted, he started to explore. He climbed up one of Olga's sleeves then spent some time wandering around her shoulders before coming down the other sleeve.

"Can I hold him, please?" asked Hans.

"Yes, of course. So long as you're gentle and don't make any sudden movements."

Hans sat beside her on the bed and she gave him the rest of the sandwich so he could tempt Aga. The rat hesitated. Instinct made him wary of strangers but he decided that, if this human was a friend of Olga's, then he could be trusted. In any case, the food smelt good.

At first, the animal tickled Hans' hand, but he soon got used to the sensation and was delighted. Frieda initially refused to take Aga, saying that she did not like his long tail, but eventually decided she did not want to be left out of the fun and, gingerly at first, held him in her hand. He soon won her affection.

Hans could not stay long because he had homework to do: he had to learn some of the catechism and write an essay about the Roman foundation of Cologne. Boring and boring. He did as little as he thought he could get away with and then wrote to Fritz. Tired, he went to bed, but lay awake for a while wondering why Olga had looked at him so strangely when he had said, "I wish I had a long tail."

***

Several days later, Hans received a reply from Fritz. There was lots of news about his old friends and teachers and he devoured the information greedily. Fritz wrote:

> *Last Thursday, Mom and Dad took me to the cinema. When we came out, there was chaos everywhere. Fire engines rushing past and clanging their bells. Police cars with their lights flashing. And the SA all over the place. But, above it all, there was this great fire and large clouds of smoke. As you will have*

*guessed, it was the Reichstag fire. You
will have heard on the radio that it was
started by a Dutch Communist, but
everyone here knows that the Nazis
started it themselves and that van-
whatever-his-name is an incompetent
lunatic who could not even light a
church candle by himself. But, in the
name of the Blessed Virgin Mary, please
do not tell anyone that I said so. None of
us are safe these days.*

> *Your good friend for always,*
> *Fritz*

Hans' first thought was, Yes, you are a
good friend, and his second was, I bet those
nasty stupid blackshirts did do it.

A Child of Cologne

8

Sophia's Story

It was not until his fourth or fifth visit next door that Hans plucked up the courage to ask Olga the question he had been dying to ask all along: why was her grandmother African?

To his embarrassment, Olga laughed and said, "Because her parents were African!" Then she became more serious. "Why don't we go downstairs so you can ask her yourself? It is a really amazing story that I never tire of hearing. It will be so much better if she tells you herself."

A few minutes later, Sophia began. "I was born in what I still think of as German South-West Africa. Some people may now call it something else, but it will always be German South-West Africa to me. I'm proud to be an African and I'm proud to be a German –

despite all the things the brownshirts did to my tribe, the Herero.

"My father was the chieftain of our village and so was a very important man. I was his only child and very spoilt. There was nothing he wouldn't give me if I wanted it. By the time I was eighteen, I was beautiful – but the problem was, I knew it. I was the chief's daughter and I was beautiful! On top of that I was also clever – or so I thought. I'd come top in every exam at the mission school, beating all the boys. There weren't any other girls in my class because the adults, including my father, thought education was bad for girls. But I'd wanted to go to school so much he had given in.

"Now I was grown up, Father wanted to marry me off. He hoped that a strong young man would be able to control me better than he had done. So he presented me with a list of four boys from the village – Abraham, Jacob, Joseph and Isaac – and told me to choose. I rejected them all. None of them was good enough for me. No boy would have been good enough for me. I must admit, I was a really horrible girl!

"Around this time, a lion took several of our goats. Then it got worse …" Sophia hesitated.

"What happened?" asked Hans.

"Anna was a pretty three-year-old. One day she was innocently sleeping on the riverbank while her mother was washing clothes nearby. They were completely unaware of the lion creeping up. Then her mother heard Anna scream. The whole village heard the screams, but it was too late. I'll never forget the look on that woman's face: a look of not only grief but also guilt. She had no reason to feel guilty, but I never saw her smile again.

"The next morning, the whole village gathered outside my father's hut for an *indaba*. The young men were eager to form a hunting party and seek revenge. However, my father raised his hand for silence and shocked everyone. He called forward Abraham, Jacob, Joseph and Isaac and said that whichever of them could kill the lion single-handed would marry me. To decide who could try first, they were to race round the perimeter of the village.

"If you think that I sat there, wondering which of them would become my husband

and worrying whether any of them would die in the attempt, you'd be wrong. As I said, I was horrible. I was too busy being furious with my father. He had tricked me and trapped me. How could I possibly refuse to marry someone who had risked their life for me?

"But then my fury turned to unease. Why weren't they back yet? People were getting restive. Finally, my father sent a servant to look for the runners. The man came back saying he'd seen them running away from the village and disappear over the top of the *koppie*."

Hans broke in again to deride their cowardice and to ask what a *koppie* was. Sophia explained that it was the name given to small rounded hills that are quite common in southern Africa. She then continued the story.

"After some time, they did come back. My father had them beaten, but they wouldn't explain their behaviour. Then I pestered them until they admitted the awful truth: they were prepared to face death but not a life with me!

"After this fiasco, my father quietly called in the help of a professional hunter, someone he'd heard was a crack shot and would have no trouble getting the lion. So, one day, a strange man came to the village. He was different. He was older than the young men who had been chosen for me. He was tall, he was handsome, and he had a rifle. This made him appear stronger than any of the men from my tribe – they had only spears. However, the most striking thing about him was that he was white. I was used to white priests, but this was the first white person I'd come across that I could think of as a man. I took one look and realised that here was the waterhole my thirsty body had been seeking. My father introduced me to him. He was Siegfried Muller from Cologne, the white hunter who had been invited to rid the village of the lion.

"That evening, there was a great feast to welcome him. All the way through, I kept stealing glances at Siegfried and, each time I did, he seemed to be looking back at me intently. After the feast, he retired to the visitors' hut and I went to see my father. I told him in no uncertain terms that this was the man I wanted as my husband and my father told me in equally definite terms that I could not have him.

"More angry than I had ever known him, he said, 'What are you thinking about, my child? You have only just met this man, and he is almost a complete stranger to us. As if that were not bad enough, he is white and no white man is going to marry you. He might want you as his mistress, but you would not want that – and I certainly would not allow it. You are a good mission girl, and my daughter. Do you have no respect for me, for your mother or for your village? Go to bed and stop being so stupid.' I didn't stay to hear any more, but went to bed.

"Siegfried went to see my father late that evening and was told all that had happened; about the lion, about Anna, about my behaviour and that of the young men of the village. Siegfried told me he had laughed at that – he understood what the young men had done, but he was in the grip of an emotion stronger than fear. He said that he'd then sat there in silence for a long time, knowing his thoughts were absolutely ridiculous. Common sense had shouted for him to stop, but he found himself telling my father he would leave at first light. He asked for two strong young men to be guides, adding, 'Their main job will be to bring the carcass back. Whether it will be the carcass of the lion or of me is in the hands of God.'

"The next morning, about two hours after dawn, I saw two men walk into the village carrying a body between them. I was very, very afraid. Then, some way behind, came a third man. He was carrying a spear in his left hand and had blood running down the ragged sleeve covering his right arm. He was able to walk almost erect, but he took faltering steps to reach me. Siegfried collapsed at my feet.

"He was carried into the visitors' hut and, at once, I went to nurse him. Once he had recovered somewhat, he proposed. I was overjoyed and accepted. Since he had killed the lion, I had little trouble persuading my father to give his approval."

"It's a pity Wagner isn't still alive. He'd have made a great opera out of that."

"Yes, and Smetana would have made a lovely one out of my wedding. It started with a full nuptial mass: long and solemn and beautiful. There were people who did not approve of my marriage then, there would be others later, and there are still others even now – but during the ceremony I knew that we had God's full approval and that was what really mattered. I clearly remember the pride I felt when my father led me into the open area beside the great baobab tree for the first dance of the festivities, and how my beautiful mother looked at me with such great love. I'm ashamed to say that, until then, I hadn't realised how much my parents really loved me."

Sophia stopped and burst into tears.

Olga took her visitors by the hands and gently led them from the room. Outside, she said, "I'm sorry about that. Sometime after Grandma sailed for Germany, Von Troth and his cursed brownshirts shot her father. They shot Abraham, Joseph, Jacob and Isaac. They shot all the men of the village. The butchers raped many of the women and then killed them too. Grandma may be proud to be a German but I'm not. How can I be after all they did to her village – and to so many other Herero villages?"

Hans was confused. He had never heard anyone say anything unpatriotic before, but this sounded horrible, so maybe she was right. Frieda got up, put her arms round Olga, kissed her on the cheek and quietly said, "I am so sorry."

9

Friendship

Maria told Wolfgang that she had caught their children visiting the half-caste girl who lived next door.

Wolfgang's response was to shout at his wife. "I don't want Frieda making friends with that mischling girl! And I will definitely not tolerate Hans making friends with her. Can you imagine what the people at work would say if they found out? Go and fetch them so I can make myself quite clear – especially to that boy. You can't be bringing them up properly, or they'd never even think of going into that house. Goodness knows what they'll have picked up in there!"

Hans and Frieda followed their mother into the lounge where their father was waiting, his belt in his hand.

"You've been a very stupid boy and, what is worse, you've taken your little sister somewhere she should never have been. However, I don't want to beat you; it would give me no pleasure. So, I'm going to be lenient – provided you promise never to mix with that girl again."

Hans' face flushed red with anger and then turned white with fear. When he had regained sufficient control he quietly said, "Olga is our friend, and I'm not going to stop seeing her." He could hear himself saying the words but, in his head, they seemed a long way off. How could he speak to his father like this? It could not be real. But the pain he felt a moment later was only too real. Blow after blow from the belt landed on his head and body until a worried Maria put herself between her husband and her son and Hans took the opportunity to escape.

Frieda tried to comfort and nurse Hans. Somewhere, she had heard that a cold compress was good for bruises, so she dipped a spare petticoat in cold water and applied it first to Hans' cheek, which seemed particularly bad, and then to his forehead. Hans grimaced but then smiled gratefully.

"Do you feel up to talking yet?" she asked after a while.

Hans nodded

"I thought you were very brave standing up to Dad like that, but we won't be able to visit Olga anymore." Hans tried to respond but Frieda didn't notice and continued. "If we defy him and people think that Olga's family are encouraging us to disobey our parents people will turn against them because they are not showing the respect for authority that the Nazi's want to see. People won't accept them anymore."

Not for the first time, Hans thought proudly that his sister was wise.

"She's the only friend I've got, too." Frieda hesitated a moment before adding, "Except you."

Hans blushed and tried to stutter an apology, but his sister kept talking.

"I can see Olga within limits at school but we need to think of somewhere for you and her to meet. What about the zoo? She often goes there because her grandfather gave them lots of animals so they let her in whenever she wants to go."

"Yes, I know, but they let her in free and I can't afford the entrance fee, not with the miserable amount of pocket money we get from Dad."

"What about a park?"

"If we go to one nearby we're likely to be seen by people we know. And if it's further away, they'd ask why I was going so far when there are perfectly good parks much closer."

The siblings sat in silence for a while.

And then Frieda had a brainwave. "Why not meet at the cathedral?"

"That's a stupid idea! Lots of people who go to there might know us. It would be like walking into a lion's den."

"Not if you do it intelligently. I don't think the priests will bother you, and lay people usually go to pray at set hours. If you vary the times you meet, they won't take any notice. They'll think you've met accidentally. Everyone knows Olga often goes to meet her father there, and what could be more natural than a good Catholic boy like you visiting the cathedral from time to time?"

"Sorry, you're right. It's not a stupid idea. You're a genius." After another short silence he asked, "What did you mean when you said that you can only see Olga within limits at school?"

"On the first day at the convent, other girls in my class pulled my pigtails at playtime. Olga came over and told them off. Then she stayed with me and that frightened them so they left me alone. However, near the end of playtime, Fraulein Mannheim, who's a cow and looks like a horse, called Olga over and said to her, 'You ought to know by now that the nuns don't like girls spending too much time going round in twos. You must go and find someone else to be with.'

"Olga said, 'But Frieda's only just come to our school and I'm trying to help her fit in.'

"Fraulein Mannheim replied, "Don't answer me back. You're too bold." And promptly gave her a detention."

"Why do the nuns object to girls going round in twos?"

Frieda had no idea. Hans was old enough to know why the priests objected to boys going around as couples, but that couldn't possibly apply to girls, could it? Then, as if a light bulb had gone on in his head, he thought, *Girls are much more attractive than boys – and much nicer. If I were a girl, I'm sure I'd fancy other girls more than boys.*

***

The next Thursday, after school, Hans hurried to the cathedral and found a seat near the shrine. He sat there impatiently for ten minutes and had decided she was not coming after all when he saw her hurrying down the aisle.

"Sorry I'm late! One of the nuns from school was coming out of the west door just as I was coming in. She stopped to talk to me and I couldn't, politely, get away too quickly. Frieda's told me how brave you were, standing up to your father. Thank you for doing it, but you mustn't get into trouble again for me. I'd never forgive myself."

Embarrassed, Hans said, "Oh, it was nothing. I'm not going to let my father tell me who I can and can't have as friends. Anyway, thank *you* for taking such good care of Frieda."

"You're very fond of her. I wish I'd a brother like you. It's a bit lonely at times, being an only child – even though my parents and grandmother are very kind to me, and I love them to bits."

"How are Agamemnon and your grandmother?" Hans realised that he had said something silly and inappropriate. She seemed to have that effect on him.

Olga simply smiled and said, "They're both very well. I'm sad that you can't come and see them for yourself, but maybe things will change. The Nazis may not be in power very long."

"Do you come here often?"

"Yes. My father spends a lot of time here – even more since the Nazis sacked him from his post at city hall. He draws and paints pictures of this tomb and the windows and all the other lovely things here. I come and visit him. I'll take you to see him, if you like."

"Do you draw and paint?"

"I prefer to draw people."

"Would you draw me?"

"Yes. I'll do it next time we meet."

For the next hour, the two children talked of this and that, of their pasts and their hopes for the future. Hans was fascinated, finding out more about Olga's past, her parents and, in particular, more of her grandparents' colourful history. She told him how Siegfried had walked through the centre of the city arm in arm with his new bride. Many people had stood and stared at the tall, beautiful, exotic couple but few had dared to say anything. Siegfried's exploits in the African jungle were well known, and he was a local hero –especially because he had collected so many animals for the zoo. No one felt like criticising him openly, and many admired this latest example of his great courage. Olga admitted that, after her grandfather had died, her grandmother had suffered from some racial abuse and so had her father.

"My family has been lucky, though. My grandfather's reputation still protects us to a certain degree. The people I'm sorry for are the Rhineland bastards."

Hans was startled to hear this word from his friend. "Who are the Rhineland bastards?"

"Oh! Don't you know? While the French were occupying the Rhineland, some of their troops fathered children with local girls. Some of the mothers were little better than prostitutes, but quite a lot were raped. They included girls from quite respectable families. Some babies were secretly aborted but, of course, the Catholic girls couldn't do that. Some parents have stood by their daughters but not all. What makes the situation worse in the eyes of many people is that lots of the fathers came from places like Morocco."

"So, people think that many of the Rhineland bastards are partly African, like you. They must be having a hard time now."

At this point, the cathedral bell rang out the hour. Hans had intended to leave at least fifteen minutes earlier to make sure he was home before his father. "My God!" he exclaimed – and fled without another word. He ran all the way as fast as his chubby legs would carry him, and managed to sneak in just in time.

Later that evening, he found an opportunity to tell Frieda what had happened and how ashamed he felt about his loutish behaviour. She agreed to pass on his apologies and arrange another meeting – for a Saturday when he might not need to rush off quite so quickly. Hans was very grateful for his sister's help and she was very proud of her important role, secretly finding it exciting.

***

The next time, Olga took Hans to meet her father straight away. They found him sitting in contemplation of the Gero Cross, the simple Byzantine-style crucifix that had inspired Cologne worshippers for a thousand years. Herr Muller welcomed him.

"So, you're the young man I've heard so much about. Would you like to see some of my work?"

"Yes please," Hans dutifully replied.

"I've not tried to copy this cross. Deep inside me, I somehow feel that it's not right. At least, not yet. The time may come. Meanwhile I'm content to just look, pray and absorb."

He then showed Hans paintings and drawings he had done of the Dombild triptych with its depiction of Cologne's patron saints, Saint Ursula, Saint Gereon, and the three kings. Olga had told Hans that Ursula had been a British princess who had taken eleven thousand maidens on a pilgrimage to Rome, only for them all to be massacred by the Huns at Cologne on their way back. Olga was sure the story must be true because hundreds of their skulls were stacked in the crypt of the cathedral.

Hans expressed admiration and this inspired Heinrich to bring out his collection based on the *Dreikönigsschrein* itself. Most were of the three wise men adoring the baby and presenting their gifts, but others reproduced the tomb's golden images of Old Testament kings and prophets and its representation of Christ's baptism. Despite initially being lukewarm, Hans became more and more impressed by Herr Muller's work. There was more to it than skill; there was something he could not put a name to. When he asked to see more, the painter said, "I'll show you more next time. I understand my daughter's going to do your portrait – if you're not careful, there won't be time."

So the young couple moved to a quiet part of the building. Olga told Hans to sit, settled herself in front of him, a sheet of paper clipped to a board on her lap, and proceeded to draw. As she drew she answered Hans' questions about her father.

"Yes, he does sell some of his work to tourists. It doesn't bring in a lot of money but it makes him feel better now that he has not got a proper job anymore. He doesn't like selling them to foreign tourists, though, especially Americans and the British because they persist in asking what he thinks of the Nazis. They are not bad people and mean well, but it puts him in an impossible situation. He obviously can't say that they are wonderful, but if he criticises them he can't be sure that the tourist won't turn out to be a fascist sympathiser or a newspaper reporter who will quote him. Such reports would probably get sent to Gestapo headquarters – and you know what that would mean. He usually pretends not to understand English."

After a while Hans felt uncomfortable. He was getting bored and was worrying about the time. But Olga would not let him look at the picture till it was finished. At last, she was done and told him to close his eyes. When he opened them it almost seemed as if he was looking into a mirror – a mirror that was deeper than any he had ever looked into before. He was too moved to know what to say and did not want her to see the tears forming in his eyes, so he held the picture up, turned around and, once again, left without a word. He did not run, but walked thoughtfully up the aisle.

Outside, still dazed, he lost his footing and slipped down the last few steps, clutching the drawing. Next to his outstretched hand, he spotted a ten-mark note. He grabbed it quickly, got to his feet and walked home. On the way thoughts rushed through his mind. *This drawing is so special. It is a perfect likeness and has brought me luck. If I had not been carrying it I would never have seen the money. More money than I have ever had before. How can I look after it? I'll stick it on the right-hand side of a piece of stiff cardboard and fold the other half over it to keep it clean.*

And that is what he did.

***

The next time they met at the cathedral, Herr Muller showed Hans more of his work. Pictures showing the colours of the windows, the towering graceful lines of the pillars and the beauty of some of the statues. Hans admired them but thought that, in some cases, the copies did not and could not match up to the originals. To avoid having to make the same sort of comments again, Hans asked Heinrich if he remembered the first time he had ever come to the cathedral.

"Yes!" replied Heinrich. "I was four and bewildered. My father had just died. I couldn't understand where he had gone, despite all the grown-ups' explanations. My mother, Olga's grandmother, brought me to the cathedral for the funeral. Father Josef, my father's brother, ushered into our seats at the front. Most of the service passed me by in a wave of tedium. If I craned my neck, I could see the archbishop standing in the pulpit that towered ahead of me. He spoke. He told the large congregation what a great and good man my father had been and said that, of all the gifts he had bestowed on Cologne, the best and most beautiful was my mother Sophia. I felt like shouting out my agreement but I'm glad I didn't because that would have interfered with that he had to say next. He said that he was very pleased to see me there, and that he was sure that I'd grow into a man of whom my father would have been proud. I don't think I've lived up to that, but I've always tried to."

Heinrich told Hans that he had been an altar boy. "There was tight discipline, but we were working for God so everything had to be perfect. It was a loving, caring discipline." Then he added, in a whisper no one else could hear, "It was nothing like the harsh, cruel discipline I endured in the army during the war."

Olga and Hans went off to the semi-secluded spot they had made their own to tell each other what had happened since their last meeting. Hans was less excited than before and this meeting was less satisfactory than the previous ones: after a while, they had run out of things to say – and much of what Olga did say he had heard already, either at their earlier meetings or from Frieda. Just before it was time to leave, he suggested that next time they should meet at the zoo.

"But I thought you couldn't afford it."

Hans told her about the ten marks, and about what he had done with her drawing. When he saw how pleased she was, he was cross with himself for not mentioning it earlier. They agreed a day and time and then Hans left – but not, this time, without saying *auf Wiedersehen.*

A Child of Cologne

10

The Letter

I t was the day before Ursula was due to leave her family, and she was going to do her last voluntary cleaning shift at the cathedral. It was a task she had enjoyed doing over the past ten years: before all the visitors arrived, there was a special kind of peace about the place. She got up early and went downstairs to make a cup of tea before getting dressed. The postman could not have come yet but there was an envelope on the doormat. It was addressed to 'The mother of Olga'.

Curious, she opened it.

> *43, Wilhelmstrasse,*
> *Cologne*
> *20 February 1933*
> *Come and see me at 10 AM precisely.*
> *Maria Smit*

Ursula smiled and said, out loud, "No way! Even if I wasn't going to the cathedral, I wouldn't follow that woman's orders."

Sophia heard her, and came down to see what was happening. Ursula showed her the letter. Sophia did not smile. She was silent for a while.

"I'll go," she said. "It's too dangerous to make enemies these days."

At 9:59 precisely, Sophia knocked on her neighbour's door. It was answered by a rather plump, dowdy woman with an aristocratic face and cold penetrating eyes. Sophia surmised that she was deeply unhappy but that it would take an earthquake for her to admit it.

"What are you doing here? I need to see Olga's mother, not ... not ..." Maria searched for a suitable word but ended lamely with "... y-you!"

"I'm proud to be Olga's grandmother and whatever you wanted to say to her mother you can say to me. She has had to go out but has agreed that I should come round."

"All I want to say to you and to your *mischling* family is that I won't tolerate my son associating with any of you – and certainty not with that girl. I know what you blacks are like. Sex mad. She'll be luring Hans up to her bedroom and seducing him so he makes her pregnant and she can demand he marries her."

If you only knew what she does entice him up to her bedroom for, Sophia thought. But what she said was, "Don't be ridiculous! Are you blind as well as stupid? Olga is not black! She's as blonde as her mother. And she's only ten years old!"

Sophia turned on her heels and, without another word, strode away.

Maria stared after her, speechless.

The next morning, the family stood on the station ready to wish Ursula Godspeed. Not for the first time, she noted how magnificent it was – and yet how small it seemed, nestling as it did in the shadow of the cathedral.

A Child of Cologne

11

The Zoo

Hans' next letter from Fritz contained lots of news about his old school and his old friends – but Hans was less interested than before. They all seemed to be part of a previous life. They were like shadows or a dream. Fritz also told him about the latest outrages committed by the SA and SS, and of the goings on in Nazi high command … but much of it seemed to be repeated from previous letters. There was one new story Hans found amusing.

We've just got a new teacher who's an ardent Nazi. On his first day at the school he spent the lessons teaching us how wonderful the Führer is and how wonderful his ideas are. Towards the end of the day, he showed us a large swastika flag he had folded up in the corner and said we were to march around the

*classroom behind the flag. Then he said,
"I don't know you yet, so I'll let you
choose which one of you is to have the
honour of carrying the flag." Without
hesitation, with one voice, we shouted
out "Anna Herzog!" The joke is that
she's the only Jewish person in the class.
He'll be livid when he finds out.*

***

Hans fidgeted as he waited for the tram
which would take him to the zoo. At last, it
arrived and he scrambled aboard. It took him
through many unfamiliar parts of Cologne.
Those ugly swastikas seemed to be flying
everywhere. He arrived to find Olga already
outside eagerly waiting to show him round.
Hans offered his ten-mark note, but the
gatekeeper refused. "Any friend of Olga's
should regard himself as a guest of the zoo,"
he said.

When Olga asked him what they should
visit first, he promptly replied "Oh! The
monkeys please." He had not been to a zoo
before, but he had heard about them from
other boys and he was not disappointed. It
was great fun watching the monkeys

scampering and chasing each other all over their enclosure. The animal's faces had such human-like qualities and they seemed to be enjoying life so much. Olga bought a packet of peanuts. She poured them into a little wagon with a piece of string attached to the end; the monkeys pulled the string and then were able to greedily devour the peanuts. Hans excitedly filled another wagon and felt an illogical sense of achievement when he saw the monkeys eat 'his' peanuts. Olga laughed when the monkeys did things that people were forbidden from doing in public, but that was when Hans wished he had another boy beside him: boys enjoyed talking about things like that – it was just embarrassing with a girl there.

Olga then took him to see the lions. There was a majestic male, named Siegfried after her grandfather, four females and a number of sweet young cubs running around. Hans enjoyed watching the pride but thought they ought to have had a bit more space. But he kept the thought that, in Africa, they would have had large areas to roam around freely to himself. After that, they went to see the bears – both brown and polar – the seals being fed, the zebras and the giraffes. The elephant surprised Hans. And not even because it was so much bigger than he had imagined it would be, but because people were being allowed to ride on it. When Olga asked if he would like a ride, Hans was thrilled. Once he had got on he was not so sure – it seemed a long way down! He soon forgot his concern as the magnificent creature took them on a leisurely rolling stroll around the zoo. He felt on top of the world.

During the visit, Hans saw some other animals that he thought did not have enough room. They were cooped up. But he kept quiet. Then he saw the leopard in a cage less than four metres long and two metres wide. It was pacing up and down, up and down. Bored, bored, bored and unhappy. Hans could keep quiet no longer.

"This is outrageous!"

Olga was startled. "It's not as cruel as it looks. The zoo is building a more suitable enclosure, but it takes time. Don't feel too sorry for him: if he were not here in this cage, he'd be dead. I'm sure, if you could ask him, he'd tell you that he'd rather be alive."

"I'd rather be dead than in prison. How can you defend the monsters who've imprisoned this majestic animal? Look at its lovely grace. He should be stalking prey in the African bush or climbing trees. He was made to hunt and catch, not to be trapped and imprisoned!"

Olga fought back her tears and did her best to defend her friends, the keepers, but Hans did not want to listen and strode off. She kept up with him, talking all the time, but he did not say a word. The tram came, she got on and he followed. It was almost empty. She moved down the aisle to the front seats and took the right-hand one nearest the window. Hans hesitated and then took the left-hand window seat, sitting in silent anger throughout the journey.

*****

"How did you get on?"

Hans' anger had subsided somewhat, but it came bubbling back as he told Frieda about the visit, in particular when he dwelt on the plight of the leopard. "I'm never going to the zoo again, and I don't want to have anything more to do with that girl!"

Frieda sympathised. "It's not right to treat any animal badly, but Olga is your friend. Just because you don't agree with her doesn't give you the right to be unkind. You should send her a note to apologise."

"Never!"

A few days later, he decided again that his little sister was wise beyond her years and sat down to write.

Dear Olga,

I'm sorry I was so nasty to you on the way back from the zoo. I'm still cross about the leopard, but I know I should not have taken it out on you. I shall never go back while they have that animal cramped up in such conditions. But I did enjoy a lot of the visit. Thank you for showing me the funny monkeys and so many beautiful creatures and also for the exciting elephant ride.

I would like to see you again but not at the zoo, and I have to admit I'm getting a bit tired of the cathedral. It is splendid but when I'm there I feel a bit like the leopard: it is vast but I feel restricted. I am not supposed to run and everyone speaks in subdued voices. It's all right for girls but it's not a place for boys. What about meeting in Elm Trees Park? It is fairly handy. I know we said

that we would not meet in a park but I
cannot think of anywhere else to suggest.
Looking forward to seeing you.

Hans hesitated, wondering how to end a letter to a girl. He settled for 'Best wishes, Hans' and then handed it to Frieda for delivery. Before she left, she read it through in front of him. Hans guessed she was thinking that he should have put a row of kisses at the bottom … but neither of them said anything.

A Child of Cologne

12

The Herman Twins

Hans reached the park just as Olga arrived from the opposite direction. He held his hand out to her shyly and formally. She shook it warmly and then embraced him. Hans was suffused with embarrassment and felt even more shy, but he managed to stutter, "Sorry I was so nasty to you."

"You're forgiven – this time," Olga responded.

"But I still hate the way your friends treat that leopard."

A moment later, he was on the ground.

As he got up again, Olga shouted, "I no longer forgive you!" and raced downhill towards the lake shouting, "You can't catch me."

Hans ran as fast as he could, but his short stubby legs were no match for hers. He saw her disappear behind the grove of trees at the lakeside but, when he reached them, she was nowhere to be seen.

"Boo!" She jumped out behind him.

It felt as if his skeleton had jumped ten centimetres while his skin had stayed still. This girl embarrasses me so much, so why am I so happy in her company? Well, most of the time?

Olga took his hand and led him to a park bench. She pulled the drawings she had done since they had last met at the cathedral from her satchel. Some were of her parents and her grandmother and there was even one of Agamemnon that she let him keep. Others were of people in the cathedral, including priests and nuns. Hans was particularly impressed by the one of Cardinal Shultz, a person they both admired greatly because of his brave condemnation of the Nazis. Although he thought the drawings were very good likenesses, the ones Hans liked best were the caricatures. Many were of clerics he knew – some he liked and some he disliked – and the way Olga had caught their idiosyncrasies brought a smile to his face. Then she showed him one of a large – very large –man in uniform wearing lots of medals. Hans froze.

"Put that away at once. You'll get us arrested." He was frightened. He also thought that what she had done was not right. Admittedly Goering was a Nazi – but he was different to the others. He was a war hero and had shot down many enemy planes. Olga put her drawings away and Hans did not tell her what he was thinking about the Führer's deputy. He did not need to; she had guessed.

Their talk moved on to other things. As they sat there, Hans could not help noticing how long her legs were. That was how she had managed to beat him, even though she was only a girl. He could also not help noticing that they looked … rather … nice and felt embarrassed yet again. Just then, on what had been a clear day, a cloud seemed to come over the sun. The youngsters looked up and saw the *Hindenburg* on its journey to New York.

"When I grow up, I want to fly an airship," said Hans.

A cloud larger and darker than the one from the Zeppelin crossed Olga's mind.

A little while later, they heard voices singing the Horst Wessel song. Two youths wearing swastika armbands appeared from behind the trees. Hans recognised them – it was the bullies known as the Herman twins. Herman Tyrann and Herman Feigling were not related but had been born on the same day and everyone feared them. Hans and Olga got up simultaneously to make their escape, but they were too late.

"I see you're making friends with a mongrel," said Herman Tyrann. Hans wanted to hit out but decided that would only make matters worse: both Hermans were bigger and older than him.

Meanwhile, the Feigling boy pushed Olga against a tree.

"There's only one thing this sort's good for!" he snarled.

Suddenly, his face twisted and he doubled up in pain, clutching a very vulnerable part of his body. The other twin looked round to see why his companion had cried out. Hans seized his opportunity and hit Herman Tyrann on the nose with all his strength.

"You've made my nose bleed! You've made my nose bleed! You'll pay for this!" he whimpered, holding an increasingly red handkerchief to his nose.

Hans found Olga's hand in his and the pair ran back up the hill, not stopping until they were sure they were not going to be followed.

"Where did you learn to do that?"

"Oh! Mother decided a long time ago that I'd need some help to survive in a hostile environment." They stood for a while in silence. "I'm not going to put you in this situation again. We must stop meeting. I'll always remember and … love you." With that, she bent forward and kissed him on the cheek.

Hans watched her run, watched her running away, but this time he did not attempt to follow. He had been torn in two. Half of him had gone away and he felt as if the other half had been powerless to stop it. "Goodbye, my love," he whispered.

***

Frieda cried when Hans told her what happened.

The next day, she sought Olga out in the playground. "I'm sure Hans would be thrilled if you did a self-portrait for me to give to him. It's not his idea – he's a boy and they have too little imagination."

Olga hesitated. "I've never even tried! Artists like Rembrandt have done some wonderful studies of themselves. But I don't think I've sufficient skill or experience. No. It's a nice idea but it would be too difficult."

"But please! You don't know until you try. And Hans would be so pleased. I would too. You're still my best friend."

Reluctantly, Olga agreed saying, "All right. Seeing as you put it that way. But don't blame me if it turns out to be terrible."

For days, Olga worked with mirrors all around her. Attempt after attempt found its way into the wastepaper basket until, on the sixth day, she had something which she felt she could describe as 'very good'.

It was then Olga's turn to seek Frieda out and give her the portrait.

"Wow!" said the younger girl. "Jesus, Mary and Joseph! Hans will be amazed."

When Frieda got home, she found Hans, told him she had a surprise for him, and handed him the drawing. She was surprised and deeply hurt when he showed no emotion on receiving his gift. He simply took the picture without a word and went to his room.

Once there, he burst into tears. He found the folder he'd made, opened it, placed the self-portrait face down on top of her drawing of him, and put them back in his drawer – together and protected front and back by thick cardboard.

Years later, he would take them out to put in the inside pocket of his Luftwaffe uniform.

A Child of Cologne

13

Magda

Ever since Magda Tyrann's parents had joined the Nazi party in 1927, they had been putting pictures of Adolf Hitler on their walls. However, for every photo of the Führer there were two of Ernst Rohm. It was his ideas, his belief in the German working class, and his hatred of the bourgeoisie that had attracted them to Nazism in the first place.

Magda felt great pride when her father was dressed in his brown stormtrooper uniform. He looked so handsome and powerful. It was even more wonderful to watch him marching through the streets of Cologne with his comrades. She could see Jews, intellectuals, communists, Catholics and all the other traitorous scum cowering in fear of the new masters of Germany.

Hitler had been in power for somewhat over a year when, one hot night in June, Magda crept downstairs for a drink. As she passed the living room door she heard her parents talking and stopped to listen.

"Our glorious leader …" Magda could not believe the tone of voice in which her father had just spoken those words. Surely he could not possibly have meant them sarcastically? But then he continued, "Hitler is far too soft and is a coward. He's not acting decisively enough against our enemies."

"I couldn't agree more," her mother replied. "But what can we do, short of having a second revolution?"

Magda stood transfixed. There was a pause, during which she held her breath.

"You mustn't tell this to a living soul. I'm not supposed to tell anyone, but I know I can trust you with my life, my love. The second revolution is coming soon. I've been told to be ready at the beginning of July. We're sure of success. The SA's two million members will overwhelm the Wehrmacht. I don't know how many soldiers it has, but I do know it's much smaller than we are. In any case, we're the men of tomorrow – they are yesterday's men. I don't know why Hitler's so frightened of them. Once our beloved Ernst is the nation's leader we will never again have anything to fear."

The girl had heard enough. She crept back to bed, without a drink, and could not get back to sleep.

Over the next few days, Magda felt a tide of rising excitement which she knew she had to keep hidden. The first day of July arrived. She would not have to wait much longer. School seemed boring and irrelevant in view of the earthquake that was about to come but she had to go, nevertheless. Eventually, the school day was over and she rushed home.

As she entered her home she felt a cold, funereal silence. Her father was home, her mother was sobbing quietly and there was a fundamental change to the decor. There were no longer any pictures of Ernst Rohm on the walls.

"What's happened? What have you done to Herr Rohm?" she asked breathlessly.

The slap her father gave her hurt, but worse than the pain was the puzzlement. He often beat Herman and sometimes, when drunk, even beat her mother but he had never before hit his sweet Magda.

"You are never to mention that name in this house again!" In a strange, high-pitched voice he repeated, "Never!"

The silence returned and remained for almost the entire evening. Magda noticed that her parents ate very little. Even Herman ate less than usual, although it was still twice the amount Magda usually ate.

Towards bedtime, her grown-up sister Helga came home from her shift at the hospital and went straight up to her room. Magda followed her. She had not dared ask her parents any questions but surely Helga would explain what was going on.

Magda found Helga sprawled across the bed, weeping. She climbed onto the bed and put her arm around her sister, comforting her until, eventually, the sobs died down enough for her to feel able to ask what had happened.

"Rohm is dead. And I'm glad he's dead. The Führer was right to have him executed. I hope he'll have his body cut up into little pieces and fed to the dogs."

Magda lost her patience. Her parents had told her nothing and Helga had only deepened the mystery. "For God's sake! Tell me what Rohm's supposed to have done."

"It's not a case of what he and his friends are supposed to have done but what they were planning to do – and what they were actually doing when they were arrested."

Magda could guess what they were planning to do.

"So what were they doing?"

"A lot of them were in bed together!"

"I don't understand. What's wrong with that?"

"Oh, Magda! They were having sex."

"But how can men have sex with each other?"

Magda felt a rising tide of revulsion as her sister, the nurse, went into detail.

"Earlier this evening, Daddy said that the name of you-know-who should never be spoken again in this house and I now agree. It must have been terrible for our beloved leader to have been betrayed by someone he thought was his friend and a loyal supporter. Thank goodness *he's* always moral and honest and trustworthy! Thank goodness he's staying as our model – not that viper! I think we should all redouble our efforts to serve him to show our gratitude."

"Yes, yes! I couldn't agree more. We must put the past behind us because tomorrow belongs to Herr Hitler – and to us."

The girls lay in companionable silence but Magda couldn't share her thoughts, not even with her sister and friend. Rohm may have behaved very badly but I still believe he was right to hate the middle classes. I'll always hate them for the way they look down their noses at us and flaunt their wealth. They're not all that different from the Jews. All the girls who come top in my class have bourgeois parents who probably do their homework for them. I hate them all. One day I'll have the opportunity to humiliate them the way they humiliate me. I don't know how yet, but it'll be great when the day comes.

Magda admired her big brother and the way he and his 'twin' dealt with the stuck-up snobs who dared to cross their paths. She was exultant when they came home and told their tales about beating up a communist or Catholic or, in particular, a Jew. At least, she admired him until the day he came home blubbing with a bloody nose. His weakness was unforgivable. That evening she had, again, gone up to Helga's bedroom to talk.

"I want to get revenge for the humiliation our family has suffered today, but what can I do? I'm only a girl."

"We girls have more power than you think. Men appear to be in charge but, when we play our cards right, we are. The secret is to remain focussed on whatever you really want and to go for it. Never be weak. It's sometimes a good tactic to *appear* weak, but that's when it's most important to remain strong and focussed inside. If you start wanting a particular man, his approval or, even worse, his love, you're lost. I should know. I've not told you before, but I fell in love with a doctor a couple of years ago. When I became pregnant, he wasn't interested and I had to deal with the problem myself. I hate men!"

"I don't see how what you're saying will help me get revenge."

Magda sat in awe as her adorable sibling outlined her ideas. From time to time, she added extra details of her own which Helga welcomed and incorporated into what she called the 'master plan'. Magda suggested that it should be called the 'mistress plan' and Helga laughingly agreed.

14

Magda's 'Victory'

Hans could not understand why this girl, one he had previously hardly been aware of, kept crossing his path and speaking to him. At first she had only grunted "Hello," but, in time, she had changed it to, "Hello, Hans." When he discovered she was a sister of one of the twins, he was even more perplexed. Now it was happening so often that Frieda had started gently teasing him about it.

"I think she fancies you."

Georges was more direct. "She's a bit of all right. I reckon you're in with a chance there!"

Hans wondered what they would say if they could the smile that lit up her face when she passed him and he was on his own. It was a smile he could not get out of his head – and it was not the only part of her that kept coming into his mind. At night, when he lay awake thinking about her, he noticed disturbing, pleasurable changes in his body. *I must not do this. It's wicked, it's sinful*, he thought. But still he continued.

Finally, he had to admit that he could not defeat temptation alone and decided to tell the priest about his wicked thoughts, hoping that would solve the problem. So he confessed all to Father Ignatius. Hans waited breathlessly for the wrath of God to descend on him but all he got was a penance of twelve *Hail Marys* and an admonition not to do it again. He left with the startling impression that his priest, the one that had taught him the catechism, had been blasé, as if he had heard similar stories a thousand times before. But, surely, that could not be the case.

Even as he walked back from confession, he was thinking of Magda again – Father Ignatius' admonition had already disappeared from his mind. The only difference was that thoughts of her smile had receded and thoughts of her body had advanced. What was particularly obsessing him were the twin pinnacles of his desire, her breasts. Hans had not seen a woman's breasts since he was a baby. He was curious, but this innate need to touch and hold Magda's face was more important. It did not make sense, but he could not help it. If going to confession had failed to cure him, what hope was there? It was not as if she had been displaying them provocatively: her clothes were modest and maidenly, she appeared to be as sweet and demure as a proper German girl should be. *She may be a Nazi, but she's obviously not like her brother.* Hans wondered what she thought about him.

A few days later, Hans saw Magda ahead of him and caught up with her. He was alone and she gave him one of her brightest smiles. After they had taken several steps side by side, Hans felt Magda's hand hold his. Her action sent a shiver of fear and joy through his whole body. Hans was tongue-tied and Magda said little till they reached her home when she saluted and said, "Heil Hitler! Hans, I think you're wonderful. Will you take me out?"

Hans could not speak, but it was an affirmative silence.

lease meet me at the entrance to the Elm Tree Park at four next Sunday. I'll be thinking about you till then."

Once again, Hans could not reply but knew that, without having spoken, he was going on his first date since Olga – and that his new girlfriend was a Nazi.

***

By half past three on Sunday, Hans was completely ready for the fifteen-minute walk to the park. He had polished his shoes till they shone. He had brushed and brushed his hair. He had even brushed his teeth after lunch – a thing he had never done before.

He reached the park a good quarter of an hour early and kept telling himself that she would not come. Why would a bobby-dazzler like her be interested in him? If he prepared himself for disappointment he would be less upset when she did not appear but, if she did come, he would be extra pleased. Or, at least, that was what he tried to argue himself into believing. Nevertheless, he kept hoping. As the nearby church clock struck its fourth note, she came round the corner. She was even more beautiful than he remembered.

What Hans did not know was that Magda had spent twice as much time as he had getting ready – and made twice the effort. He had wanted to look his best; she had wanted to look her best without it being obvious that she had done so. She was aiming to be seductive without looking like a trollop and had tried on a succession of blouses that revealed varying degrees of cleavage. In the end she had gone for one that was low but not too low. Similarly, she had raised and lowered the hemline of her skirt several times and had ended up leaving it above the knee, but not much.

Hans still felt somewhat tongue-tied, but this time he took the initiative and grabbed her hand in his as soon as they met. He felt it important to show that he was the man and in charge. He guided her down the hill towards the elm grove, aiming for the bench just beyond: the one on which he had sat with Olga. As they reached the trees, he found Magda guiding him into a clearing. It was completely secluded, even the entrance was obscured from the casual passer-by. Once they were inside, Magda sat upright on the grass and Hans sat beside her. Immediately he put an arm round her shoulders and tried to kiss her.

"Please don't, Hans. I've never been kissed before and want to wait. Can't we just talk?"

Hans was taken by surprise. When he had told Georges about his forthcoming date, his friend warned him that she had been out with a number of other middle-class boys in recent months and had left them all humiliated. Georges could not or would not go into detail, so Hans had told himself that it was all lies and Georges was jealous. As a result, he had decided that he did not want Georges as a friend anymore. But, even though he did not believe Georges, he was very surprised that a girl as attractive as Magda had never been kissed. Still she should know, shouldn't she? But now Magda was whispering to him and he was all ears.

"Hans, I've been dreaming of being alone with you like this for ages. Ever since I heard how bravely you dealt with that nasty brother of mine and his cowardly friend. You're so manly. Is it true that you plan to be a pilot when you grow up?"

Hans admitted this, saying, "I wanted to fly airships, but the recent tragic disaster means I've decided to fly Messerschmitts instead."

"You'll be a wonderful ace, and shoot down lots of enemy aircraft."

108

Hans decided she was not only beautiful, but also a very deep thinker.

"But I'm very worried about you."

Not just beautiful and clever, but caring as well. What more can I ask for? Hans thought.

"I'm worried that you were with a mulatto when you hit Herman. Do you still see her?"

"No," he said, glad he was able to reply honestly. But then he added the lie. "And I never think about her."

"Good. I wouldn't want you spoiling your life with that piece of rubbish."

Hans squirmed but remained silent.

"Now we've cleared that unpleasant business up, you may kiss me. I couldn't bear to be kissed by a man who was thinking about another girl, let alone one thinking about a subhuman."

Hans put his arm around Magda again. This time she twisted towards him and moved her face forward until their lips met. Hans knew immediately that this was no first kiss, but he was beyond caring. At last Magda was in his arms and kissing him passionately. They lay down and Hans kissed his sweet, adorable girl on her lips, on her cheeks, on her ears and on her eyes while she murmured in contentment. After a while, she sat up.

"I'm feeling rather warm. Do you mind if I undo the top button of my blouse?"

When she settled down beside him again Hans could not resist the temptation. He undid the second button, and then the third. And then he slid his hand inside. He was unable to see the smile of triumph that crossed Magda's as he struggled to undo the buttons.

"Please be gentle with me. And don't touch my nipples – at least not yet."

The boy took lots and lots of pleasure from touching her breasts. More pleasure that he had ever known before in his life. But it was not enough. His hands strayed from the tops of her breasts towards her nipples increasingly often: she gently guided them away every time. Then, in one quick movement, she rolled away from him and got to her knees. She slowly and deliberately undid the remaining buttons of her blouse and took it off. Hans lay where he was, bewildered and stunned. But she stretched down her hands, pulled him up until he knelt before her, and placed his hands over her breasts. Hans devoured her nipples with his fingers and then with his mouth. He thought he would go mad with happiness. But it was still not enough. He wanted more. Then … then her fingers were not touching his face, they were not undoing her buttons, they were undoing his. They felt within his trousers and Hans was liberated. He was free. Before that moment, he had not realised how desperately he needed to be freed from the confines of his trousers. And then … then she started touching him again. He wanted her to never stop. But she did.

"I could only go with a boy who was a true German. Do you love Adolf Hitler more than Jesus?" she whispered.

"Yes! Yes! Yes!" he cried. Nothing mattered any longer. Nothing except that she continue doing what she had been doing. And then … The end came with great relief, with great pleasure, and yet a feeling of dissatisfaction. He did not know what he had been expecting, but certainly not this mess.

And certainly not the picture that came to his mind. A picture of a girl's face – Olga's face. She seemed to be trying to speak but no words came, just a sound like a cockcrow. Hans rolled onto the ground and, three times, moaned Olga's name.

Magda heard him, got dressed and walked away muttering, "I'll destroy that evil mongrel bitch. Sterilisation's not enough for a bastard like her."

15

Kristallnacht

O n 8 November 1938, Matron summoned Nurse Nachtigall to her office. "Nurse Braun has come down with a severe fever and, so she will not be able to represent our hospital at the lecture to be given by Doctor Fischer of the Kaiser Wilhelm Institute for Anthropology, Human Heredity and Eugenics in Cologne tomorrow. As you can imagine, she's very disappointed. You will be very pleased to learn that I've chosen you to go in her place."

Ursula was trapped. If she let slip – by word or gesture – that she was not pleased with this honour, unwelcome questions would be asked. Silence would be yet another betrayal of Ilse, Bal and all the children of mixed race. She kept silent and hoped for a miracle.

But a restless night brought no miracle and she made her way to the station, catching an early train in the hope of being able to see Father Mathias before the lecture started. At a number of stops along the line, Ursula noticed there were fires in the town but she could not see which buildings were burning. At one stop, she saw armed Gestapo officers herding a group of battered and bleeding Jewish men into an empty carriage.

After arriving at the hospital in Cologne, Ursula sought out Father Mathias.

"How are you, Ursula?" he asked, "And how are Heinrich, Sophia and my little Olga?"

"As far as I know, we're all well. I'm planning to give her a surprise this afternoon by collecting her from school and spending some time at home before I have to return to Rhöndorf."

"But what's brought you here today?"

"Matron has sent me to attend the lecture and report back to the other nurses. I was reluctant, but could see no sensible alternative. And reporting back seems a betrayal too far. I want your advice on what I should do – and, even more, I need your blessing for whichever path I decide to take."

"The government's actions are wicked and quite contrary to the teachings of Mother Church. Many brave priests have denounced them and been sent to concentration camps as a result. However, it's made no difference whatsoever to the Nazi views and behaviour. All their sacrifice has done is lead to the tragic loss of good men we can ill afford to lose!

"You do know, don't you, that Balthazar was amongst the children that the Institute took away and sterilised without using anaesthetics? It's a great pity you've not been able to watch him grow up. He's a kind, intelligent young man who was full of life until they took him away. Now it's as if a light has been switched off."

The news revolted Ursula and made her feel even more guilty.

"You know you will always have my special blessings whatever happens."

Ursula left contemplative and found a discreet seat near the back of the hall. From her vantage point she saw Father Mathias arrive – and Nurse Tyrann, who now wore the uniform of a ward sister. A man who she presumed was Doctor Fischer sat on a dais beside the matron of the Cologne hospital. The woman rose.

"Before I introduce this afternoon's speaker. I am pleased to make an important announcement from the Gestapo." She recited the rest, partly from memory and partly from a sheet in front of her. "At five minutes to midnight last night a message was sent out to all our units ordering them to destroy Jewish shops and burn down their synagogues. A fine of one billion marks is being imposed on the Jews to pay for all their hideous crimes. I've just heard that our brave guardians have been carrying out their orders faithfully throughout the morning, and have also arrested thousands of Jewish men who are to be sent to concentration camps."

She sat down while the hall echoed to cheers.

16

Ursula's Stand

As Ursula Nachtigall sat in the high, coldly clinical room, waiting to find out her fate, she saw episodes of her life flash by. Everything else was in slow motion; not least the hands of the clock which was the only object hanging on one of the spotlessly white walls.

The first flashback took Ursula back to the age of five. Mummy was expecting a baby. Ursula had new questions to ask every day and she now recalled how patiently her mother had answered the many questions she had raised. At the time, it seemed as if the days of waiting would never end but, at last, she was told that baby Martin had arrived and that she would be allowed to go and see him in the hospital. When Ursula saw Martin she thought he was the most beautiful thing she had ever seen and had decided, there and then, that she would become a midwife when she grew up. With a lump in her throat, she remembered that Martin never did grow up … and her nursing experience had not been confined to midwifery.

The second occasion she remembered was the precise minute when her life had taken the left fork in the road: the moment she had seen her Heinrich for the first time.

Her third memory was of a time, years later, when the Rhineland was occupied by French troops. Ursula was sitting down to dinner with her parents and siblings when there was an insistent banging on the door. She rushed to open it and found her school friend Ilse crouching there, dishevelled and with blood running down her leg. The girl was distraught and her speech unintelligible, but Ursula and her mother helped her upstairs to the spare bedroom. Ursula's memory of her friend's distress was vivid but, at the time, she had not known what had caused it. The next morning, Ilse had haltingly told her what had happened as she walked home from her grandmother's. She had come across a French soldier who had been beaten up by a couple of his so-called mates and left in a ditch. She knew only a little French, and the soldier knew little German, but she treated his injuries as well as she could and they had talked. It turned out that the injuries were not too serious, the greatest damage had been to the soldier's self-esteem. His assailants had attacked him because he was a Moroccan and they were white. The nuns had always taught her to treat people in trouble with kindness. Unfortunately, the soldier had interpreted her kindness as something more. He was lonely, he had been humiliated and he needed reassurance, to know he had value as a person and as a man. He had ignored Ilse's protests and had left her in the ditch in which she had found him.

The final scene Ursula relived had taken place earlier that day but it already seemed to have been an eternity ago. The clock contradicted her feelings, showing a mere two hours had passed.

The matron had introduced Doctor Fischer, saying, "I'm sure you'll all want to hear about the great work he and his Institute are doing to protect the people of the Rhineland from negrification."

Ursula had sat in stunned silence as, all around, her fellow nurses applauded loudly. None more so than Helga Tyrann.

The doctor rose to his feet. "Heil Hitler. Matron has been too kind in her introduction. I'm only doing my duty for our beloved Fatherland, just as you're all doing your duty by bringing good, clean, healthy Germans into our world. My job is to put into practice the ideals enshrined in our Führer's law for the prevention of hereditarily diseased offspring. We made a good start by sterilising syphilitics and other mentally subnormal idiots. Now, you'll be relieved to hear, we have sterilised all four hundred of the Rhineland bastards."

Ursula vaguely heard a great cheer go up and then found herself on her feet. How she had got there, she did not know – but worse was to follow. She screamed at the speaker: "And you did it without anaesthetics!"

The matron had slowly risen and given orders "Sister Tyrann, please escort this traitor to my antechamber and leave her there till I'm ready to deal with her."

The green light over the door went on to summon Ursula. Two burly men in double-breasted trench coats were standing there,

one on each side of the matron. The Gestapo
were waiting.

A Child of Cologne

17

Olga Seeks a New Sanctuary

When Olga came out of school that day she was met by Father Mathias. She had only met him a few times before but he had shown a particularly strong interest in her. She thought this strange and had once asked her father about it but he was embarrassed and quickly changed the subject which was not at all like him.

The priest stood in front of her in silence for some time before saying, "I'm afraid I have some bad news for you, my child – about your dear mother." He went on to tell her about the conversation that morning and what had happened in the lecture. "I've made enquiries and discovered that she had been last seen being escorted by the Gestapo to their headquarters in Cologne." He gave Olga his blessing and returned to the hospital.

Olga went home – to find her grandmother dead and the house devastated by fire.

***

After the fire engine had gone and her grandmother's body had been removed, the spectators drifted away and Olga found herself alone. No one attempted to comfort her. She drifted far out in her sea of misery for a long time but, at last, there was a lighthouse. At first she did not see him, she only sensed his presence. Then, slowly, the invisible fog that had enveloped her lifted and she jumped up to fling her arms around her rock.

"Oh, Daddy! Oh, Daddy! They've murdered Granny and taken Mummy away! We have no home. What can we do?"

She felt her father's arms tighten around her and a tender kiss on her forehead. Heinrich gently eased her down and sat beside her on the doorstep, his arm around her shoulders. He said nothing. Olga knew he was praying for guidance – but the only prayers she could find were ones full of angry questions.

After a while, he got up and guided her through the remains of their home. The front room was gutted. It was nothing but a blackened, wet, smouldering mess populated by the skeletons of furniture, pictures and memories. This where her grandmother would have been when the fire started: she would have been keeping an eye out for Olga coming home from school. *Maybe if she'd not been in that room she could have escaped,* Olga guiltily thought.

They moved into the dining room. It was not quite as bad, but was still uninhabitable. The sofa and easy chairs were badly scorched and the dining room table was burnt. The room still felt hot, but that would soon change because the disappearance of the windows meant the cold autumnal air was free to get in. However, the worst thing was the smell. It was sickening and insufferable – and there was a whiff of petrol.

The kitchen surprised them. It was out at the back of the house and in a much better state. The electric cooker did not work, the lights had fused, the walls were black and there was soot everywhere, but the chairs and small table were intact.

The upstairs windows had not broken, despite the heat, so Heinrich opened them to cool the rooms. Here too, they were faced with soot and dirt and debris. Olga could not see a way forward: the mist returned.

Heinrich took her by the hand and led her back to the kitchen. "We'll make this our base camp for the time being. Tonight, we'll eat what food we can salvage. Then we'll go upstairs and change the bedding: the clean sheets should have been all right in the linen chest. It'll be dark soon, and you're too tired to do more than the minimum tonight, so we'll start to clean up tomorrow. And I'll go out and buy a primus stove and some. Meanwhile, I think an early bed is called for. You'll need all your strength to face the days ahead. Your mother ..." Heinrich stopped for a few moments before continuing, "... has some sleeping pills somewhere, I'll find them and give you a couple." He rose from his chair to go and look for them.

"Please, sit down, Daddy. I've something to show you." Olga took the letter out of her satchel and handed it to her father. "I'm sorry. I wasn't going to show it to you, at least not yet, but I can't keep it to myself any longer."

Heinrich sat down to read it. "I don't understand. Who's this 'friend of Agamemnon'?"

"Hans. I'll explain about Agamemnon some other time – it's not what's important now. What matters is that he's very involved with the local Hitler Youth and he wouldn't have risked sending a message unless it was serious. He's taken a big risk for me – and so has Frieda because it must have been her that put it in my satchel. Hans may be a Nazi now but he's still being a good friend." After a few moment's hesitation she continued, "I don't know why I showed it to you. There's nowhere for me to escape to. I couldn't go to Rhöndorf: they'd easily find me there. Where else is there for me in Germany? No other country would have me. In any case, I couldn't leave you, especially now. I'm sorry, I'm sorry! It was very selfish of me to show you that letter. You can't help. I've just added to your worries and that's the last thing I should be doing now. Please forgive me."

"Of course I forgive you, my darling daughter. You were quite right to show it to me. At the moment, I don't know what we can do but I'll have a think about it. And I'll ask Father Josef and the other priests for advice."

I'm glad I didn't tell Daddy who or what Agamemnon is, Olga thought. I very much hope an answer can be found soon. Whoever attacked our home today may well return to finish the job off.

What she could not have known was that Magda and Herman were keeping a low profile. They knew well that the Gestapo took a poor view of people who acted on their own initiative instead of simply obeying orders.

The next day, Heinrich returned from the cathedral with the news that all the advice his friends could offer was to suggest that they should move in with one of them. Olga's immediate reaction was to refuse: endangering people at the cathedral was not an acceptable solution. Heinrich agreed. In fact, he had already turned down their offers. So for the next two weeks, they camped out at 41 Wilhelmstrasse, worrying that each day might be their last. But then, one day, Heinrich found a possible solution.

"I heard one of the priests saying that the Quakers are organising trains to take children to England. Maybe we can get you on one of those."

"That sounds wonderful. But I can't go. I couldn't leave you here alone. I could never desert you."

"I think you should. But let's sleep on it. Important decisions are best made in the cold light of morning."

Although she took sleeping tablets again, Olga did not sleep well. In the small hours, she became aware of someone else in her room. It was Sophia! Her grandmother was no longer the charred, shrivelled husk of two weeks before; she was once again the strong, vibrant woman Olga had always known. It therefore seemed perfectly natural to hear her speak.

"You don't want to desert my Heinrich. I'm proud of you for that – and grateful – but please, think again. Hans used to tell you that Frieda was wise beyond her years. I can see you're surprised I know, but it's a grandmother's job to understand these things. Anyway, now I want you to be wise beyond your years and realise that this is best. It's not only best for yourself but also best for your dear daddy, your mummy and even for me. We need to you to survive. Our lives continue in yours. We'll survive through you. Please, take this wonderful opportunity to escape. It's still your choice but, whatever you do, may Our Lady and all God's holy angels guard and keep you."

Olga was not aware of her grandmother leaving but saw the grey light of morning penetrating the bedroom curtains.

***

Some days later, Olga and her father stood in a queue that stretched for several blocks from the offices the Quakers had set up. The Hirstman family were behind them. Solomon was a tailor from whom Heinrich had been buying suits for many years – although not many because they were high quality and lasted a long time. Solomon described how, on 10 November, a gang had wrecked his shop, broken all the windows and destroyed all his stock. How could the countrymen of his father and of Beethoven, Brahms and Goethe have fallen to such depths? Olga listened, and relived her own walk home that terrible night.

"There's no future for Jews in Germany," Solomon's wife, Ruth, added. "That's why we're trying to get our daughters out. I only hope there are places left when we get to the front of the queue."

Heinrich had thought this too, but had kept his fear from Olga. Eventually, however, the Mullers and the Hirstmans got to the offices and Olga was handed the precious permit that would allow her to travel to England in five days' time.

Much of the next five days was spent in packing and repacking the one small suitcase that was all she was allowed to take. There was much agonising. Which cuddly toy? In the end she rejected the expensive Stieff teddy bear in favour of Jumbo, the moth-eaten old elephant her mother had bought for her at the zoo when Olga was very small: he would bring back many memories. Clothes were a problem too, but she decided to concentrate on taking ones that would help her keep warm through the coming winter because the summer of 1939 seemed a long way off. The one thing there was no question about was her portfolio of portraits. It contained pictures for which her parents and grandmother had patiently sat and ones of Hans and Frieda which she had done from memory.

Heinrich and Olga took the opportunity to revisit many of her favourite places. They went to the zoo. Olga was disappointed: the place had never felt the same since her visit with Hans and, now, the expectation that she would never see it again left her feeling as if nothing was real. A visit to the cinema to see *Snow White and the Seven Dwarves* was more successful. It made them laugh and want to sing so much that they forgot their troubles. As they came out into the daylight Olga found herself wondering if one day *her* prince would come but, that night she had a nightmare in which Nazi Germany was a wicked stepmother. They went for walks in the park where the knobbly brown chestnuts covered the ground. On one of these walks, Olga told her father about the incident with the Herman twins. She even confessed about Agamemnon and, to her surprise, her father laughed.

"That's just like you! You've always loved animals." In return, he decided to tell his daughter about the Tommy although, of course, he made no mention of her conception.

Naturally, the cathedral was the place they went to most often and it appeared in the nightmare that filled Olga's penultimate night in Cologne. In her dream, hearing the steady drone of hundreds and hundreds of aircraft interrupted by deafening explosions, she got up and went out to see the cathedral. It appeared to be sailing, intact, through a sea of ruined buildings and debris – and the remains of many people littered the streets.

On their last day together, Heinrich led his daughter to the Gero Cross. They knelt in front of it for a long time, the vast space of their spiritual home around them. They each prayed silently that God would protect the other and that the evil cloud that darkened their Fatherland would be lifted.

As they rose from their knees, Heinrich told his daughter that he had something for her suitcase. He drew from his portfolio a painting of the Gero Cross.

"I've tried so hard, but I still can't reproduce the impression I have in my mind. It seems that I never will, but this is the very best that I can do."

"But it's perfect! I shall treasure it all my life. There will be no need for me to look at it to remember you, but I'll love having it to show it to my children and grandchildren when I tell them about the wonderful artist who was my father. Maybe … maybe, one day I'll be able to bring them here to show them the cross itself." What Olga did not say, what Olga could not bring herself to say, was that maybe she would bring them to see the artist. That was a hope too far.

After leaving the cathedral, they wandered alongside the river looking at the giant barges drifting by. There were no tourists. It was the wrong time of year. Olga looked at the river flowing on and on to Rotterdam where it would be absorbed by the vast German Sea and then by the even more vast Atlantic Ocean. She could not help feeling that her life was also flowing to Rotterdam and beyond and that it too would, sooner or later, be absorbed in a vast endless ocean.

On the morning of her departure, Heinrich and Olga arrived at the station early, but there were other parents and children there already, many in tears. Soon, a powerful, masculine-looking engine drew up pulling six coaches behind it. Some of the children clambered on board straight away in an effort to get the best seats, but Olga was amongst those who stayed with their parents until the guard's frantic whistles persuaded them to get on. As the train pulled away, she leaned out of an open window waving for as long as her father was in sight. Heinrich waved back, but was mesmerised by a mother who was pulling her child back out of an open window of the moving train. It was the tremendously dangerous act of a tremendously desperate woman. Heinrich then trudged back to what was left of his life.

***

As Olga settled down in her seat, she looked around and realised that she was completely alone. There were, of course, children in the other seats – some crying, some comforting the others – but they were obviously all related to or friends of each other. She alone had no one. Olga was a solitary Catholic in a sea of Jewish children. She had never felt so lonely in all her life and fell into a mood of dark despair. She remembered with love and loss all the people and places and things she had left behind. She did not weep, her grief was too deep for tears.

The train stopped at a station and a tremendous noise shook Olga from her introspection. Every other child in the carriage was shouting and cheering, and pointing at something on the platform. She looked out to see the Dutch tricolour flying in the breeze. They were safe on Dutch soil and need no longer fear that the Gestapo would stop the train. A few moments later, another great cheer welcomed Dutch women who had come on board to hand round sweets and apple cake.

When one of them welcomed her to Holland, saying in perfect German, "I hope you enjoy this cake which I made myself," the dam holding back Olga's tears broke.

That was the moment she knew she had escaped.

***

Olga fell asleep, exhausted, and saw her father. He stood in front of her holding a large object. At first she could not make out what it was but gradually it became clearer. Olga was amazed that he could hold something so obviously heavy with such ease. Then she saw what it was and understood.

The jolt of the train stopping woke her, but someone shouted, "The boat won't be ready for another hour," so she didn't move. Instead, she got out her sketchbook and drew something she had never tried to draw before, the object she had seen in her dream.

She drew the Gero Cross to her own satisfaction, to her father's standards and to the greater glory of God, our everlasting Father.

A Child of Cologne

PART TWO

Olga's English Sanctuary

A Child of Cologne

18

England

The Kindertransport organisers took Olga and the other children straight from Harwich to the Butlin's holiday camp at Dovercourt, a short distance down the coast. Once she had settled in, Olga sought out the small group of Catholics of Jewish descent and attached herself to them. Together they went to the local Catholic church where the service in Latin and the familiar rituals immediately made them feel at home. They felt sorry for the Lutherans who had problems understanding the language of the Anglican service: it was not just English, it was archaic English. But both groups were happy to see cribs and Christmas decorations that reminded them of home.

After breakfast on Christmas morning Polly, one of the helpers, wished the Christian children a happy Christmas on behalf of all the other helpers. She then sat at the piano and suggested some carols. The Lutheran group gathered round and sang *Stille Nacht*. The Catholics responded with *Adeste Fideles*. Mr Liebermann, the teacher in charge of the one hundred and thirty-six Orthodox Jewish children from Cologne's Lawne School came forward to offer good wishes on behalf of the school and the small group of liberal Jews.

The Orthodox children soon took control. Olga resented this but recognised that it was only natural because they were by far the largest group. Then she saw an older girl steal a cake from Anna, one of the younger Catholics.

"Give that back or I'll punch you on the nose!"

Although she had shouted angrily, she couldn't help but smile as she remembered Hans punching one Herman while she kneed the other. She wondered whether it was her broad grin that had frightened the other girl into returning the cake.

Upon hearing the commotion, Mr Liebermann came over and asked what was going on. Olga said nothing. The Lawne girl told the whole story, trying to justify her attempted theft by saying that Anna was not a proper Jew and so should not have been on the Kindertransport. Mr Liebermann called all the Lawne children together and gave them a lecture. Olga and her friends could not hear what was being said, but it put an end to any bullying and intimidation – although there were also few signs that any of the Lawne students were trying to like them.

Olga felt very lucky to be at Dovercourt. She was well-fed, comfortable and safe. There were plenty of activities to keep them occupied. Nevertheless, she had the feeling that she was in limbo, a no-man's land between the past and the future.

***

In the middle of January, her five Catholic friends left for London. She left a few days later with the other children, boarding the London train back at Harwich. Olga sank into a seat in an empty compartment, grateful for the chance to think about her mother and her father and Cologne in peace. Her pleasure was short lived. As the train started, three girls wearing the Lawne uniform hesitated outside the compartment door before coming in. They sat opposite Olga for some time without saying anything. One of them was glaring at her, but it was another who finally spoke.

"My name's Rebecca. These two are Rachel and Ruth. Everyone calls us the three Rs. We're part of the Lawne school, but we wanted time together, away from the others. It's a lovely school and we're very proud of it, but we do like to be by ourselves sometimes."

"We have the most marvellous headmaster ever!" Rachel said. "He's been giving us lots of extra English lessons and planning our escape for ages. Naturally, we had to keep the plans top secret and that wasn't always easy. Sadly, we've had to leave him and most of the school behind for now – but they'll be following on a later train."

Ruth interrupted "I recognise you! You're the girl who threatened to punch my nose. The Catholic with the African grandmother."

Olga had recognised her immediately but had hoped that the recognition would not be mutual. Now she was trapped. She had been in difficult situations before, but this time the odds were higher – literally three to one. Her brain whirled, racing to find the best strategy.

"When Herr Liebermann spoke to us that day," continued Ruth, "he said that the Nazis don't care what kind of Jew we are. To them, a Jew is a Jew is a Jew is a non-Aryan. And she said quite a few people in England don't see things much differently: to them a Jew is a Jew is a Jew is non-British, even if they're described as coming from here. So he told us that all Jews should support other Jews – even when they disagree. But I think that what our teacher said could be expanded to say that all immigrants should support all other immigrants."

"Thank you," Olga said quietly before getting up and gently kissing each of the other girls on their cheeks. The four stood with their arms around each other until the train jolted, toppling them back into their seats.

***

Olga had to wait on the platform in London for some time before she heard her name being called. She stepped forward the moment she heard it and, as she did so, a couple stepped out of the group of adults standing opposite. They appeared to be in their late twenties and had serious but kind faces. Once again, Olga felt her life was suspended between two worlds.

"Welcome to England," said the man. "My name is William Rowan and this is my wife, Betty. We're going to be your hosts."

Olga did not know the English word 'host', but interpreted it from the context and replied, "Oh, thank you so very much, Mr and Mrs Rowan; you're very kind."

"Please call us Betty and William. We belong to a religious group called Quakers, who believe strongly in equality and so don't use titles."

Olga could see the surprise on their faces when she said, "Yes, I know. Sorry, I mean I know Quakers address people with their Christian and surnames not that I knew you were Quakers. My father's boss was one, but the Nazis sacked her as well as him." And she burst into tears. She could not help it. But Betty immediately enveloped her in a hug.

When Olga had composed herself little, the Rowans took her to the Grand Eastern hotel. Neither Betty nor Olga were at all hungry, but William ate a hearty meal before leading them to his Austin Seven. Olga knew little about cars but had been told that the Volkswagen was better than non-German cars. However, when she got into this one, she decided that the English car was much roomier. Betty sat in the front with a map on her lap, navigating.

The car was too noisy to allow satisfactory communication between the front and back so Olga looked out at the passing scene. London was disappointing; just street after street of cheap housing. There were streets like that in Germany but one good thing Hitler had done was to replace many of them with better ones. She had been hoping to see the famous landmarks; Big Ben, Tower Bridge, Buckingham Palace and all the rest. She saw none of them. All she saw of any interest was a sign for Stratford, which she knew was where Shakespeare had been born. She recalled how much she had enjoyed playing Romeo in the school production one year.

After they had been driving for about forty minutes, William stopped the car. Betty got out and climbed into the back seat alongside Olga. William doesn't need a map-reader from here, so I thought I'd join you. I expect you're disappointed not to have seen the more interesting parts of London, but we'll find an opportunity to go sightseeing another time. Liverpool Street is in what we call the East End, and our home is in the eastern part of England. We couldn't have visited the West End, where the famous places are, without going well out of our way."

"I was pleased we went through Stratford."

Betty looked puzzled at first, but then smiled and said, "Sorry, that wasn't Shakespeare's Stratford. His birthplace is in the Midlands, about a hundred miles away."

Olga did some quick mental arithmetic and decided that must mean about one hundred and sixty kilometres. How long would it take her to get used to these strange English measurements?

There came a lull in the conversation and Olga plucked up the courage to ask Betty about Quaker meetings. "What do you do? I've heard you sit in silence for a whole hour!"

"I know you'll want to go to a Catholic service on Sundays, but you would be very welcome at our meeting if you ever wanted to come. To understand Quaker worship, you need to experience it."

"Thank you for the invitation, but I can't accept. The Church does not allow us to attend ordinary services in non-Catholic churches, except for things like weddings and funerals, we can go to those so long as we don't take an active part."

Betty smiled. "My sister, Stella, is getting married at Easter. Obviously, William and I will be going so you'll be able to come with us and see inside a meeting house. Actually, it's going to be in Jordans, which is a really historic meeting house." She hesitated for a moment and then laughed. "Sorry, built in 1688. Hardly historic in Catholic, or even Anglican, terms but it is by our standards! Some of the most influential early Quakers worshipped there and William Penn, who founded Pennsylvania, is buried there."

They settled into more casual conversation until Olga saw another place name she recognised. "Oh!" she said. "I've heard of Colchester! They told us about it at school because it has a lot in common with Cologne. They were both big Roman camps and then they were settled by retired Roman soldiers.

That's where the 'Col' comes from. And they both had had lots of Roman temples."

Betty smiled at her enthusiasm.

"Sorry about giving you that lump of history you probably know already," said Olga. "But I remembered it all when we came through on the train. We seem to have come in a big circle."

"Yes, and it gets worse. At Southolt we'll be only three miles from Manningtree and that's only a short ride from Harwich. It would have been much easier to pick you up from Dovercourt – but then I wouldn't have had the opportunity to start to get to know you during the journey."

"There's more about Colchester. I'd an uncle who was injured and taken prisoner in the war. He was brought to Colchester. Actually, I think he was looked after by Quakers. The Friends Ambulance Unit?"

"Not all members of the FAU were Quakers, but many were. It started at Jordans and they trained people there. Another circle! We've only another ten miles or so to go but, for one reason or another, we don't often go to Colchester. We tend to go to Rowell instead – it's a similar size and about the same distance from Southolt. But we'll make a point of going to Colchester soon."

Shortly after that, they passed a sign for Stratford Saint Mary – but this time Olga chose not to comment. At the bottom of a small hill, they crossed a large stream which Betty said was the river Stour and the border between the counties of Suffolk and Essex. The road climbed up the opposite side of the shallow valley to a road sign, pointing right, which said *Millford 2, Southolt 1* – a score-line Olga would remember with affection for the rest of her life.

A Child of Cologne

19

Southolt

At eleven o'clock on Olga's first day in the cottage, Betty offered her a cup of tea and some biscuits. "Now you know where you're to live, do you have any ideas about what you want to do?" she asked.

"What I'd really like to do is to continue my education, but I don't know whether that's possible."

"I don't know either, but I'll arrange for us to see the head of the grammar school." She explained that this was the only possibility because Olga was too old for the other state schools.

On Wednesday morning, the three of them were ushered into a spacious book-lined office. A large plaque on one wall bore the names of the pupils who had been killed in the war. Doctor Butler rose to greet them.

Olga studied his face and decided that she might rather like going to a school of which he was the head. She imagined that he would be more interested in helping pupils find their lost property than in punishing them.

"Welcome to Rowell Grammar School," he said. He pointed to the letter in front of him. "Thank you for telling me so much about Olga. I think she could bring a lot to us, things that would enrich the school and broaden the horizons of its pupils. However, there are serious problems to address. The fifth form will be sitting for the matriculation in six months' time and have been preparing for it over the past eighteen months." He turned to speak directly to Olga. "What's eight times fourteen?"

Taken by surprise, she was confused and hesitated. Her brain told her that she could multiply eight by seven and double the answer. Unfortunately, her mental arithmetic went wrong somewhere so she replied, "One hundred and six."

"Almost every child in this school would have instantly answered one hundred and twelve because they've been brought up knowing that there are eight stones in a hundredweight. They're also used to the idea of working with the fact that there are thirty-six inches in a yard and sixteen ounces in a pound. It might be peculiar, but it does gives a much better grounding in number than always relying on decimals."

Olga felt humiliated, and was angrily trying to understand how one hundred and twelve was the same as a hundredweight when she heard the next, apparently simpler, question.

"What foreign languages have you been taught?"

"English, thank goodness!"

Doctor Butler congratulated her on her mastery of the language and then said, "We learn French here. Do you know any?"

"Only *égalité, liberté, fraternité* because the first letters spell ELF which means eleven in German. In Cologne, we start preparations for the carnival to celebrate the departure of the French after the Napoleonic Wars on 11 November each year."

Betty sensed a metaphoric drop in temperature when that date was mentioned and involuntarily lifted her eyes to the plaque. The fourth name leapt out at her and she wondered if Captain R.E. Butler was a relative of the head.

The latter quickly brought the meeting to a close, saying brusquely, "I had a meeting with the chief governor before you came and we agreed that it probably wouldn't be appropriate to allow Olga to join the school. I've heard nothing this morning to change that view." He rose and escorted them from the premises.

That evening, at a post mortem on the meeting, Olga pointed out that the head had been very warm and welcoming when they arrived but was almost hostile when they left. "Was it something I said that caused the change?" she asked.

Betty told her not to blame herself: she couldn't have known that 11 November was such a significant date in Britain. Olga apologised anyway.

"Well," said William, "since it seems Olga won't be going to school, what will she do?" Other possibilities were considered and quickly dismissed. Any vacancies in local shops, bakeries, farms and so on would inevitably be filled by local girls whom the employers had known for their entire lives. Nearly all jobs further afield required skills Olga had not yet acquired.

The three sat in contemplative silence for some time.

"I could train her!" Betty exclaimed. "Teach her typing, shorthand, simple bookkeeping, filing and all the other things needed to be a good secretary. I could spare an hour or so a day and I think she would learn quite fast."

"I'd love that! Thank you so much. We did learn a little typing and bookkeeping at the convent school, but not a lot. Unfortunately, they taught more shorthand than anything else. German shorthand will, I think, be little use here. However, what Betty can teach me will be useful, I'm sure."

***

On Saturday the Rowans took Olga to Rowell. She was delighted to see a small Roman Catholic church on the far side of Southolt village. They stopped so that Olga could make a note of the times of mass and the priest's name. She asked about the saint the church was called after.

"He was an English king, better known as Edward the Confessor, who died nearly nine hundred years ago and was responsible for building Westminster Abbey," explained Betty.

"He was also responsible for the Normans invading," added William.

"Ignore him, he has a bee in his bonnet about 1066, the Normans and the aristocracy. If you don't hear more about 'the most important date in English history' from him soon, I expect others will tell you about it."

Olga did not have the foggiest idea what her two new friends were talking about but decided to keep quiet. William stopped the car again outside what looked like some kind of shop. The sign said 'Fish and Chips'. Olga followed Betty and William in. They both asked for cod and sixpenny-worth of chips with salt and vinegar. When they asked her what she would have, Olga decided that the simplest thing was to copy them. She watched, incredulous, as the food was wrapped in newspaper. Surely that must be unhygienic. However her hosts did not bat an eyelid and she trusted them. Eating fish and potatoes fried in hot fat was a new experience, but she decided the food was actually quite nice.

The first place they visited in Rowell was a splendid old bookshop quaintly called 'The

Ancient Bookshop'. The building was lavishly decorated with white plaster designs that William said was pargetting. He added, proudly, that it was unique to that part of the country. They were there because William and Betty intended to buy her a small library of appropriate books. The nearest public library was here in Rowell, so it would be better for her to have a stack of her own, at least for the time being. Since her knowledge of English literature was limited, Olga could take only a small part in the decisions about what should be included. They agreed that her collection must include pocket-sized booklets on English wildflowers and trees and a slim volume of English history. For poetry, the obvious choice seemed to be Palgrave's *Golden Treasury*, and Lamb's *Tales from Shakespeare* was added without much discussion. Fiction was more difficult. It seemed desirable to include a selection of English female authors, so Jane Austen's *Pride and Prejudice* and Emily Bronte's *Wuthering Heights* went on the stack. William and Betty felt that the problem with many male authors – including such classically British writers as Robert Louis Stevenson, Sir Walter Scott and H. Rider Haggard – was that their stories had too much violence. But Thomas Hardy's *Far from the Madding Crowd* and Charles Dickens' *David Copperfield* were amongst those they deemed acceptable, despite the latter's slimy Uriah Heep. To lighten the load, they included *Alice's Adventures in Wonderland* and the *Just so Stories*. The couple firmly excluded standard works that they judged Olga was likely to find heavy going. The proscribed list included *Robinson Crusoe*, *Pilgrim's Progress* and *Vanity Fair*. William suggested J.B. Priestley's *English Journey* but Betty disagreed.

"It's too political," she said. "Let's leave our friend with some illusions about England, at least for the time being." In its place they agreed on the Suffolk and Essex volumes of Arthur Mee's *King's England* saying they might add other counties later. When they left the bookshop, all three were heavily laden, so they retired to a nearby Lyons tea shop for afternoon refreshments.

After going back to the car and leaving the books, they went down the road to the Odeon to see *Snow White and the Seven Dwarves* – Olga chose not to mention that she had seen it already, albeit in German. For the

160

next week William, Betty and Olga all found themselves singing *Heigh-ho* from time to time, and Betty could sometimes hear Olga plaintively singing *Someday my Prince Will Come* in the solitude of her bedroom.

***

In the months before the war, Olga lived quietly in Southolt. She helped Betty with what little housework was needed and went with her to the village shops. At first, she found the unfamiliar brand names on the forest of tins and packages bewildering, but she soon managed to distinguish between them. It took much longer to get used to the strange kinds of bread and meat, but only then was she promoted to shopper-in-chief. There was a lot of curiosity in the village and she had to field many questions in the early days. Betty had warned her that the people of East Anglia were not generally known for being welcoming to strangers, but Olga decided that most of those in Southolt had made an exception for her. When she thought about it she concluded that the anomaly could be explained because they saw her as young, alone and thought that she looked vulnerable, and, besides, she was living with the Rowans. William was the village solicitor and he dealt efficiently and discreetly with many of the inhabitants' most intimate affairs. They liked and trusted both him and Betty. Thanks to Olga's help in the home Betty was able to act as William's secretary more often.

At first Olga did not notice but soon became aware that there were more visitors speaking strange accents or even foreign languages in the village at weekends than during the week. She asked Betty about this and was told that they had come to see the place because one of England's most famous painters, known locally as John C., had been born there and many of his most famous paintings were of nearby scenes.

***

Daily life at Apple Cottage had a comforting routine. Breakfast was often porridge followed by toast and marmalade. Betty made lunch. The components of the meal were different each day but varied little week by week; for example, if it was Monday then Olga would expect to see the minced remains of the Sunday joint. William came home to eat it and usually took Betty back to work with him while Olga washed up, tidied the place and did whatever chores needed doing. Betty was a good cook and liked to mastermind dinner so, later in the afternoon, Olga might do some of the unskilled preparation – peeling potatoes, for example – leaving her host to demonstrate the culinary skills she had learned from her Northern mother: they all enjoyed consuming the results. Finally, around ten o'clock, William would bring in cups of Bournville cocoa and plates of bread and cheese for the three of them to share before bedtime. Olga looked forward to the days when a new tin of cocoa had to be opened because, nestling in the top of each tin, wrapped in tissue paper, there was a small animal made of coloured lead. Each had a name, and there were stories about them in a magazine issued by Cadbury's for the 'Cococubs' who collected them. Olga knew that she was really too old for such childish things but she had brought so little with her from Cologne that she coveted these absurd creatures. The line of them on her mantelpiece grew even though, occasionally, there were duplicates that she put away in her drawer.

Having grown up over the past six years without the guidance of her mother, and with a grandmother who had been the daughter of a chief and then the wife of the game hunter Siegfried, Olga had not learned to knit. Upon discovering this gap in Olga's education, Betty set out to fill it – and to also teach her how to darn and crochet. While sitting quietly and employing her new skills, Olga would think of those she continued to love although they were dead, missing or a long way away. She also thought about some of the things she had been studying: English shorthand, English history, English literature and English language. In the last of these, she had been particularly delighted to learn the sophisticated word 'philately'. William had used it when he had brought down the album of stamps he had collected as a boy. She had never seen a stamp collection before and was surprised by the wide variety of subjects depicted. There were ones showing almost every kind of African animal; beautiful flowers, butterflies and birds from every corner of the world; and portraits of kings, presidents and dictators. As she turned over the pages, she noticed that the section for Germany included a stamp bearing the infamous legend '1 million marks'. She knew it must have been issued around the time she was born, during the era of hyperinflation. She was very impressed with the collection but felt no desire to take up the hobby herself, even when William told her that the king was a very keen collector.

On Sundays, Olga went to mass at Saint Edward's. The Irish priest, Father Michael, and many people in the congregation made her very welcome, but others had an innate mistrust of incomers in general, foreigners in particular and Germans above all. They remembered only too well what Germany had done in 1914 and what they could see was it starting to do again. At first she had been puzzled that her reception in church should have been cooler than in the shops – but then she realised that the big difference was the presence of Betty during her early visits to the village. Olga felt that there was a subtle difference between how people reacted to her in England and in Germany. There, people had thought she was not really German, whereas, here, the problem was that they considered her to be thoroughly German. She wondered what the attitude of the Southolt inhabitants would be if she looked more like her father's mother. As Olga continued to worship with her fellow Catholic villagers she was increasingly accepted.

Monday afternoons were set aside for a letter to her father. For his safety, she sent them under cover to his uncle, Father Josef, at the cathedral. She was not sure whether or not the Gestapo opened them and so carefully avoided saying anything at all political. She got a letter back each week but they were even more bland than her own. Before she had left, Olga and her father had agreed four secret code words which he would use if there were indications her mother would soon be out of the concentration camp, if she were released, if the situation had grown even worse or if he heard she had died. She scanned the letters carefully each week, but none of the code words ever appeared.

During her free time she enjoyed reading her new books. Sometimes she would listen to the wireless. Some tasks, such as vegetable peeling or washing-up, could also be done while listening. The Home Service had an hour of broadcasts for schools at each day and often there were other interesting programmes full of snippets of information for Olga about almost anything under the sun. At other times she listened with the Rowans to powerful dramas, comedy shows, (which she often could not understand or see what was amusing) and, of course the news. This was essential listening and got steadily worse and worse as 1939 progressed.

***

Three Saturdays after her arrival, Olga was asked by the Rowans if she would like to go to Colchester and responded "Oh! Yes please, I'd love that!" and so they set off down the A12 before turning off into Colchester. As they were driving along the high street, Betty told Olga that the street and the Roman town around it had been burnt to the ground by the local tribesmen under the warrior queen called Boudicca in AD 55. Olga wanted to sound impressed.

"Wow! And what did the Romans do about that?"

"They came back, fought Boudicca and won a pitched battle. Their revenge was merciless. After that they had relatively little trouble."

"That's a sad story." But, underneath her words, Olga was remembering a history lesson at school in which the teacher had proudly told them how the German tribes, under their leader Herman had dealt with the Romans. They had lured several legions deep into the forest and slaughtered them all. As a result, Rome did not establish a proper foothold beyond the Rhine. "

They visited the castle, which had been built on the site of a Roman temple and was now a museum, and then went to the zoo before heading home.

"Thank you for taking me to Colchester," said Olga at dinner. "It was very kind of you – and very interesting."

Instinctively, Betty knew there was more she wasn't saying and asked her if she had really enjoyed the day.

After a long pause, Olga said, "You've both been extremely kind to me and I'm very, very grateful for all your care. However, I know how much truth means to you so I can't lie. On the whole, I've not enjoyed today, it has just made me feel even more homesick. Time after time I've been reminded of Cologne, but Colchester is not Cologne and that increased my feeling of homesickness still further. You couldn't have foreseen that – and, indeed, I didn't foresee it myself. It's just one of those things that happen. But, please, don't take me there again."

"We are sorry that you felt like this but appreciate you being so honest with us. It couldn't have been easy."

There was another pause.

"I'm sorry," Olga said, "but I've another confession to make. I not only compared Colchester with Cologne but I also repeatedly judged it to be inferior. The fact that the Germans kept the Romans out while the Britons succumbed made me feel superior. What's up with me that I can think like that? Haven't I seen enough of where such thoughts can lead? Years of Nazi propaganda seem have infected my mind."

"Don't be too hard on yourself," said William. "Tribalism is alive and well in England too. There is widespread satisfaction here that on maps of the world a quarter is painted pink to indicate the British Empire. Do you know that in English schools they only teach English history? And I mean English history. Even the Scots, Welsh and Irish don't get a mention – except at times when they dared to challenge England."

"We must stop getting so political and serious," said Betty. The play on the radio is about to start. The *Radio Times* says that it's an adaption of an Agatha Christie novel."

"But I thought you didn't approve of violence," said Olga. And they all laughed.

***

On Good Friday afternoon, Olga attended the Stations of the Cross service at Saint Edward's and left feeling spiritually refreshed. She spoke to Father Michael afterwards, and reminded him that she was going to a Quaker wedding the next day.

"As I said before wish you weren't. The Quakers do a lot of good and that makes them particularly dangerous. Don't let your association with them allow your faith to be undermined. Also it's not Easter until Sunday, and the Church doesn't permit weddings during Lent."

"I'm sorry to cause you concern, Father. The Rowans have never made any attempt to convert me. I know it's a Lent wedding but, since it's not a Catholic one, I didn't think that would matter."

The priest raised his hand above the girl's head and said, "Peace be with you, my child. May our Saviour, the Lord Jesus Christ, guide and protect you from all temptation."

The next morning, Olga got into the Rowan's car for the hundred-mile cross-country drive to Jordans. This time, there were no place names she thought she recognised. After almost two hours they came to a crossroads Olga where saw two signs. One pointed to Jordans meeting house, which was visible diagonally opposite, and the other to a youth hostel just beyond. Olga did not know what to say about the meeting house. She had seen the one in Rowell from the outside a couple of times and did think this one looked more like a proper church, but she could hardly say that. The words 'plain', 'simple', 'unpretentious' and 'attractive' came to mind, but they did not seem adequate for a place so obviously precious to the Rowans. Instead, she said, "Did you know that the youth hostel movement started in Germany? I've never stayed in one, but there's a hostel in Cologne and lots more all over the country."

Before Betty had time to respond, William turned right down the side road alongside the meeting house and then turned into a small space just in front of the gates to the car park. The back of the car protruded slightly into the road and the driver of a bright-red sports car honked his horn loudly as he flashed past them at a dangerous speed and disappeared round the next corner. Olga thought she heard William swear, but dismissed the idea until she looked at the faces of her two friends. The tell-tale blush on Betty's was in sharp contrast to William's pallor. Betty said that the only thing William ever swore about was his car.

"I wish they'd widen and straighten out that road. It's a death trap! There were plans to do it several years ago but then some of the great and good started writing letters to *The Times* saying this quiet and historic part of the countryside should be protected and the idea was scuttled."

The car was parked and then they walked round to the front of the building where there was a small collection of gravestones. William said that this was where William

Penn, members of his family and other early Quakers linked to Jordans were buried. He also explained that, early Quakers had stabled their horses in the area now occupied by the car park.

Betty disappeared, and William and Olga went in. She saw rows of wooden benches along each of the four sides of the room. The back row on one side was a little higher and William told her that this was the ministering stand where, in times past, those speaking would stand. In the middle of the room was an oblong wooden table on which rested a vase of daffodils, several copies of the Bible and another book. They were sitting too far away for her to be able to read the title properly, but it appeared to be something like *Christian Faith and Practice*. Betty's sister Stella and Robert Fell, her fiancé, sat next to each other on the bench facing the table. Olga thought Stella looked lovely in her simple sky blue dress and Quaker bonnet. Betty sat behind the couple with a friend of Robert's. They would act as the two witnesses for the registration of the wedding.

A woman and two men came in and sat on a bench across the table from the couple. Olga remembered Betty telling her that

Quakers had their own registrar for marriages, so she guessed that one of these three was the registrar and the others were elders. It seemed strange not to have a priest, an altar and lots of statues. There were no stained-glass windows either.

Olga and William sat together quietly while the room filled up. She was surprised that there was not a quiet buzz of conversation as people greeted their friends. Everyone seemed to be concentrating and no one seemed to look at anyone else. When all were assembled, one of the elders rose from the bench.

"Welcome to Jordans. A particular welcome to those of you who have never been to a Quaker wedding. The wedding will be part of a meeting for worship. The meeting will be silent until the couple have made their promise to each other. After you have witnessed this and listened to what has been said, you may feel guided to speak yourself. Please stand up, speak clearly and try to keep your ministry short. Do not speak too soon after someone else, and do not speak more than once. The meeting will conclude when I shake hands with Simon, my fellow elder."

Ten minutes later, Stella and Robert stood up holding hands. "Friends, I call upon you to witness that I take, my Friend Robert Fell to be my husband, promising, through divine assistance, to be unto him a loving and faithful wife, so long as we both on earth shall live." Robert made a similar solemn declaration.

Several Friends ministered, praying for God's blessing on the union. The only words Olga remembered afterwards were a quotation from George Fox:

> *For the right joining in marriage is the work of the Lord only, and not the priests' or magistrates'; for it's God's ordinance and not man's; and therefore Friends cannot consent that they should join them together: for we marry none; it's the Lord's work, and we are but witnesses.*

As she was thinking about these words, the elder stood again, shook hands with the other elder beside him asked them to remain seated while the couple left with the registrar and their witnesses to complete the legal documentation.

"While the couple's marriage is being registered you are invited to witness the promises that you have heard and what you have seen by coming forward to sign the marriage certificate yourselves," he continued. "When you have done so, please make your way to the Mayflower Barn where the breakfast is being held. For those who have not been to Jordans before it is through the new burial ground beyond the one immediately outside where William Penn and his family are buried. As you may know the barn was built in the 1620s from the timbers of a ship named the *Mayflower*. Whether it was the one that took the Pilgrim Fathers to America or not is open to question."

Olga held back for a while, wondering what Father Michael would say. In the end, she decided it would be churlish not to sign and he would never think to ask if she had done it. The certificate was not only a legally recognised document but also a work of art showing a number of things associated with the bride and groom, both from their earlier lives and since they had met. While signing it, Olga spotted a drawing of the meeting house in the top left corner and, opposite it, one of a young girl in Austrian national dress. She carried a suitcase very similar to the one Olga had brought with her from Cologne. This picture was, presumably, meant to acknowledge Stella's work for the Kindertransport.

As they made their way to the barn, Olga saw semicircles of simple gravestones, bearing only the deceased's name and dates, on her left. The large bank to her right was covered in yellow daffodils. William excused himself at the barn door because he had to collect a guest, who had been delayed, from nearby Seer Green Station. Everyone else was deep in conversation and no one came forward to greet her. She looked up at the ceiling, which she thought was like the inverted hull of a ship. It was clear that the beams had once been part of one. She wondered if it really was the famous *Mayflower* that had carried the Pilgrim Fathers. Olga was glad she had read about them in her history book. At first, she had just regarded them as another bunch of English heretics, but then she realised what an important part they had played in the foundation of New England. She now compared her lot with theirs. Like her, they

177

had been forced to leave their homes because of persecution. Their lives had also been saved by the kindness of strangers. However, they had crossed the Atlantic Ocean in sailing ships facing ship's rations, disease and many stormy days, while she had only crossed the German Sea in a steamship. But she knew she would have gladly faced the worst of storms and endured any hardship if it had made it possible to bring her beloved family with her.

A voice called for the guests to be seated and then for a silent grace. At the end of the silence, William returned with the guest he had collected from the station who sat down beside her. She was astounded when he introduced himself in perfect German – albeit with a slight Prussian accent which reminded her of Hans. His name was Corder Catchpool and he worked for the Quaker's Berlin Centre. He seemed to know a lot about the Kindertransport and asked her a lot of questions about that in particular, as well as more general ones. He asked her if she knew much about the history of German Quakers and Olga had to admit that she did not.

"There were never many," he said. "And the few there were fled to Pennsylvania in the 1680's to escape persecution and conscription. Some of them went to Philadelphia and formed a community called German Town which had its own meeting house and where the revolutionary idea that slavery was incompatible with Christ's teaching arose. At first, the Quakers already there were uncomfortable with this idea. It took many years for the American Quakers to be persuaded but they also brought the Quakers in Britain round to the same opinion. Eventually they, with the help of others, managed to convince the British government to abolish slave trading. Perhaps you can see why I feel so proud to be working for German Quakers."

On their way back to Suffolk, Betty told her more about Corder Catchpool. "He's been very outspoken about the need to respond to Germany's grievances. This has made him very unpopular in some quarters here but has won him the ear of some Nazis. He played a significant part in negotiating the Kindertransport. Maybe if the government had listened to his ideas earlier, Hitler would never have come to power."

***

After the disappointment of the Colchester trip, the Rowans were reluctant to take Olga sightseeing in London but, by the beginning of August, they were starting to think it might be a case of now or never. So, on 5 August 1939, the trio caught the nine forty-five from Manningtree to Liverpool Street and then took the underground to Saint Paul's. This visit started in another disappointment for Olga which she felt could best be illustrated by the message Christopher Wren had left behind: "If you want to see my memorial, look around." It seemed to her that the cathedral had been built more to the glory of the architect and his king than to that of God. She came out silent and depressed.

However, her spirit soared when she entered Westminster Abbey. This was the place where kings and queens had been crowned since the days of Saint Edward, a place steeped in history, but it was indeed, above all, a place where God's majesty was revered and he himself was worshipped. Olga realised that this was a place built by Catholics whereas Saint Paul's had been built by Protestants. She wondered if that would explain the difference that she felt.

The Houses of Parliament and Big Ben were awe-inspiring in a secular way. As the trio stood on Westminster bridge, William quoted the lines Wordsworth had composed on that spot. While he declaimed, "Earth has not anything to show more fair," Olga gazed at Saint Paul's from this new angle. Now it appeared to be a house of God towering above the houses of Mammon, which it dwarfed.

"Dear God!" cried Betty. "What will happen to this view if the bombers get through?"

"Not if," said William, "but when." He took each of them by the hand and led them to Lyons past the statue of Queen Boudicca, standing guard.

Amongst the other places they visited in London that day were the National Gallery and the Tate Gallery. Olga was particularly delighted to see the originals of paintings by Southolt's famous son. He was by no means her favourite artist, although Olga was not sure who was – possibly Durer. What she was sure about was that she was disappointed they had not time to see many of the drawings the galleries owned, particularly those by Leonardo da Vinci.

181

Olga knew that she had only to speak and her friends would retrace their footsteps to please her. But she was reluctant to ask because they had already cut short their stays at several other places for her benefit, amongst them Friends House, the Quaker headquarters opposite Euston Station. Besides, over the last few months, they had gone out of their way several times to allow Olga to spend time exploring a fine collection of drawings by local artists at Rowell's art gallery.

She thoroughly enjoyed her visit to London zoo, apart from feeling it was a bit disloyal to think that it might, just might, be bigger and better than the one at home. They also went to the Natural History Museum. She preferred live animals to stuffed ones but was overwhelmed by the size and complexity of the dinosaur skeleton that William informed her was not a fossil but a cast donated to the museum by Carnegie. A little further in, he pointed to some bones hanging from the ceiling of another large room. "As far as we know, the blue whale is the largest animal that has ever lived on earth."

When they got back to Suffolk, she drew some of the animals they had seen at London Zoo and in the Museum. Betty and William were very impressed by her work, so she asked if she could show them some of the work she and her father had done in Cologne cathedral.

"I'm very sorry," said William, "but not tonight. Betty's very tired and not feeling well. She needs to get to bed."

The next morning, when Olga came downstairs, William told her that Doctor Jameson had been to the cottage during the night and had prescribed several days of rest for Betty.

"Oh dear! What's the trouble? Is there anything I can do?"

"She's almost three months pregnant, but the doctor says there's a real danger she'll lose the baby. We've lost two before and he's very worried that if she loses this one we'll never have another chance. He has suggested complete bed rest."

Olga did not ask how she could help again; she knew the answer would be "anything and everything." For the next ten days or so, she worked harder than she had ever done before. Then, just after eleven

183

o'clock on Sunday, 3 September, she took a cup of tea upstairs for Betty and another for William, who she knew would be sitting at the bedside, intending to tell them the news she had just heard on the wireless. She knocked at the door. There were muffled voices and she could hear Betty crying. A white-faced William opened the door "Betty is bleeding and I have to take her to hospital immediately." She put the cups down, fled to her room, flung herself on the bed and howled. Her grief was not just for the Rowan's baby, but also for the countless numbers whose violent deaths would almost certainly follow from today's announcement of the declaration of war.

***

A fortnight later, William went with Betty to the hospital for her check-up and to find out whether she would ever be able to have a child again. Olga sat at home, waiting for their return and turning her thoughts over and over in her mind. Should she say what she was planning to say if the news was bad? Or would it just make matters worse? She did not know.

At last she heard the car and saw them walk slowly up the drive. Betty was crying. William was stony-faced and his skin was ashen. Olga rushed out to help Betty into the cottage and to her favourite chair. She knelt beside her, holding her hands in silence for a long time before saying hesitantly, "I'm very, very sad that you won't be able to have children. I know what wonderful parents you would have made. You don't have to give me an immediate answer to my suggestion, but I would be so happy if you and William could let me become your daughter. It would be so wonderful for me to think of you as Mother and Father. Of course I will always have my birth parents and will love them as Mutter and Vater. Please think about it, you don't have to answer me now."

Betty and William looked at each other and said, in unison, "Thank you, we would love that."

A Child of Cologne

20

The Hall

A month after war was declared, Betty was well enough for a trip to the Odeon to see *The Wizard of Oz*. Once again, the three of them returned home singing – *Somewhere Over the Rainbow* this time – and, once again, Olga's sleep was disturbed by a nightmare. In her dream, Olga lived in Munchkinland and the wicked witch and her flying monkeys had complete control of Kansas. She wanted to come to Munchkinland but the Munchkins were flying large balloons to keep the monkeys, the witch and her broomstick out. Olga woke in a deep sweat, worrying about whether or not the barrage balloons she had seen in London could possibly be enough to keep Hitler at bay. At least she was sure that her pacifist family did not need to travel along any yellow-brick road to find a heart: they already shared a large one.

The next day as they were having their lunch William said, "Sam Browne has asked to see me at the hall this afternoon."

"Who's Sam Browne?" asked Olga.

"He's the closest the village has to a lord of the manor – he owns Southolt Hall."

"Is that the large building that looks like a prison? Opposite the Anglican church?"

"Yes, though I think you're being a little harsh. You can only see part of it from the road and that doesn't give you the best idea of what it looks like. It's got a lot of history and character that have grown on me over the years."

"How old is it?"

"No one knows. The original records were destroyed during the Peasants' Revolt in 1388. You can find out about that in your history book. There may be a reference in the *Richard II* part of Lamb's *Tales*, too. I can't remember, but I must warn you that the Bard is about as reliable on history as Doctor Goebbels. Anyway, the hall remained in the possession of successive lords of the manor, who added to it from time to time. Then, in 1848, the last lord lost all his money through reckless gambling and sold the hall to a French nunnery who bought it as a sanctuary. They made extensive alterations: in particular, they created a chapel and brought an ornate altar from Italy to place in it. The chapel and the altar are both still there. Eventually, the nuns decided it was safe to return home and the hall passed to the Franciscans who made yet more changes. I've been told that they were much more popular in the village than the nuns who belonged to a contemplative order and kept themselves to themselves. The friars took part in village activities and made themselves useful." William got up from the table and started to put his overcoat on.

"But when did Sam Browne come into the picture?"

"Sorry, I can't stay now or I'll be late for my appointment, but I hope to be able to answer that later."

That evening, he came home with news that made them forget that particular question.

"Sam Browne asked me over because he's volunteered to join his cavalry regiment now, rather than staying as a reservist until he's called up. That means he'll be away for as long as the war lasts, although I expect he'll be allowed home on leave from time to time."

"Cavalry? Does that mean he'll be riding his horse into battle?" Olga asked.

"No. As you may have guessed, I'm not exactly the greatest expert on military matters but I understand that he'll be fighting in tanks, as he did last time. He was rather young then but this time he'll be a bit on the old side. I'd normally keep my clients' business private but he said that he was happy for everyone to know he'd enlisted."

"But what did he need to talk to you about?"

"He has requested that I take over control of the estate while he's away. There are seasoned staff who'll be able to cope with day-to-day affairs, but he needs someone to deal with unforeseeable emergencies. It wouldn't be fair to put that responsibility on his staff; he doesn't pay them enough. I'm not sure my charges are high enough to justify taking the risk either, but I don't think my conscience would let me increase them in the circumstances."

"I understand it when you're generous to your poor clients, and I approve of that, but I'm not so sure about it when it's the rich who benefit. Still, I'm not going to interfere," said Betty.

"Professional confidentiality doesn't allow me to comment on whether Sam is rich or not, but let's just say it depends on how one defines 'rich'."

Betty let the matter drop. William then turned to speak to Olga.

"He gave me another surprise. He said that he would like you to visit him at ten tomorrow morning. I said I'd bring you if you agreed to go, but he doesn't want me there. He said that I'd make the visit too expensive! I assured him that I wouldn't charge for my time but he insisted on seeing you alone. We left it that he'd expect you unless he heard to the contrary. I think it's strange. I wouldn't blame you for refusing to go."

"I've never even seen him. What kind of man is he?"

"Although he's been my client for several years I can't say that I know him. He's very quiet and reserved and looks melancholy. I think there may be some tragedy in his past but I don't know, I'm only guessing. One thing I do know is that he has no immediate family. Just an estranged cousin in Canada."

"I'm intrigued. I want to go."

"You're old enough to make your own decisions," said Betty "And you can change your mind even as late as tomorrow morning. I'm not happy about it. A man of his age ought to be married. There are enough women around who would, I should think, be only too pleased to have him. He's quite good looking – though not a patch on my Will, of course – and he appears to be pretty well off. Both things mean a lot to many women. Rumour in the village is that he sometimes visits Amelia Stubbs – or should I say Lady Amelia from Stratford St Mary. Anyway it's only because they're both passionate about horses: no man looking for a wife would consider her – she has a face like the back of a bus and a figure to match."

"That's not a Quakerly way to talk …" William rebuked her with a smile. "… even though we're always supposed to speak the truth."

***

At five to ten, Olga started to walk along the drive which led through an avenue of high ancient hedges to the main entrance of the hall. This side of the building looked much more attractive than the part visible from the road.

A man with a sad, interesting face opened the door. "I'm Major Samuel Browne," he said and led her down a short wood-panelled corridor. "This part of the hall is known as the Queen Anne wing ..." He opened the door to a large room, pointed to the ceiling and added, "... and that's by Adam."

Olga tried to appear impressed although she did not know the Adam he was talking about from the original Adam. She did, however know a little about Queen Anne from her history book. "Wasn't Queen Anne the last English queen? I mean, the last English monarch before my Hanoverian countrymen?"

"I'm impressed. I've never thought of it like that before, but you're right. I don't think the current king would be happy to have himself described as German, though! Not so sure about his brother; there are rumours that he has a soft spot for Herr Hitler. Anyway, we're well rid of him. I'm glad he abdicated."

There was an oak table encircled by eight high-backed oak chairs in the middle of the room. On the table, at the end nearest the door, stood two Wedgewood cups and saucers with matching milk jug, sugar bowl and slop basin. The tea cosy was a Wedgewood blue and the protruding spout indicated that the teapot belonged to the same set. The major drew out a chair and invited Olga to sit. He seemed to stand behind her chair a moment longer than necessary before moving to sit opposite her. Olga would not have noticed if their initial handshake had not also been longer than she would have expected from someone supposed to both an officer and a gentleman. What was more, he had also looked deep into her eyes until she broke contact. Olga tried to dismiss her uneasiness, reminding herself that she had not had long to get used to English customs and habits and had no experience of those of the upper classes.

Sam Browne's opening words of conversation were, "Will you be mother, please?" She had become acclimatised enough to respond, "Do you take milk and sugar?"

"After we've had tea, I'll take you to see the animals. There's Napoleon, Henrietta and their piglets, lots of chicks and hens ruled by a noisy cockerel, five Jerseys who produced the milk for our tea and a number of geese. At the end of the tour I'll show you our stables. We've four horses: Goliath and Samson are massive Suffolk Punches who do the farm work. I'll tell you about the other two when we get there."

Olga was delighted by the animals, the five-day old piglets in particular, although she found the aggressive tactics of the geese somewhat intimidating. However, she was really looking forward to seeing the horses. Goliath and Samson, who stood in the first stall, were just as impressive as their owner had promised. But, when Sam Browne opened the second stall, Olga was overwhelmed. There was a handsome chestnut stallion, who Sam said was called Noble, but it was the smaller one that she immediately fell in love with – the kind of love some girls instinctively feel for their favourite horse. It was an all-black mare with mischievous eyes.

"Her name is Black Magic, but we call her Magic. I keep her for visitors … although, I must confess, I don't have many of them. I presume William told you that I'll be joining my regiment soon?"

Olga nodded her head.

"The reason I've asked you round is that I'd like pictures of these two animals to take with me. William has been telling me how good you are at drawing. Would you be willing to draw my Noble, and Magic too? I'll pay you, of course. Would ten pounds for each be enough?"

Olga had never had a paid commission before, and the amount he suggested took her by surprise. "Thank you. That's very generous, but I'd rather do it for free."

"I won't hear of it!"

"All right then. I'll do it in exchange for a ride on Magic."

"Have you ever ridden a horse?"

"No, but I'd love to try."

"Come round next Tuesday. I'll give you a lesson and then you can spend an hour drawing them. Is it a deal?" He offered his hand and, once again, shook hers for a time that seemed unnaturally long.

The same happened when he gave her a parting handshake a few minutes later.

Later, she told Betty everything that had happened, including her reservations about the handshakes.

"The landed gentry are not to be trusted, especially when it comes to vulnerable young girls. I'm glad William isn't here because he wouldn't approve of a generalisation like that, but I think he's sometimes a little naïve. Just be careful."

Betty repeated her warning as Olga set off the following week, with excited anticipation but mixed with trepidation – about both the man and his beasts. In the end, riding was even more exhilarating than she had expected and, as for Sam Browne she found his quiet charm undermined her reservations. She finished the first stage of her drawings and they agreed, with another handshake, that she would return the following week to continue with her lessons and the portraits. It took four sessions for her to feel that the drawings were the best she could achieve and that they were ready to show to Sam.

"You've got them off to a T! Thank you so much."

Olga was grateful Betty was not around to hear what he said next.

"I'd like you to come up to my bedroom. I want to show you something."

She followed him to the north wing of the hall. Near the end of the corridor, he stopped at the foot of a wide sweep of stairs.

"My bedroom and office are at the top of these stairs. I want them to be private so I don't allow the staff up there. I even do the cleaning and if I say so myself they are kept spotless."

She felt that she had no alternative but to follow him up into the unknown. At the top of the stairs, he opened a door and stood aside to let her enter. The first thing she saw was a king-sized bed with a spotlessly white coverlet. Beside the bed was a photo of a girl who looked disturbingly familiar.

"That's Helen. She was my fiancée. The photograph was taken on her eighteenth birthday, the day we got engaged. Helen was altogether lovely but her most distinctive feature was her diminutive ears. I couldn't afford to buy diamonds on my pay as a lieutenant but when I saw those earrings in an Oxford Street jewellers I knew had to get them for her. In the end, I borrowed money from a fellow officer so I could give them to her as a birthday present. I wish you could have seen the sparkle in her eyes when I put them on! It rivalled that of the jewels. She immediately agreed to be my wife and gave me a kiss that was chaste yet held the promise of more, much more, when we could finally be married. She kissed me in the same way the next day as we said goodbye at Waterloo station.

"Ten days later, my CO summoned me to his office. That was most unusual and I was scared stiff, even though I couldn't think of anything I'd done wrong. To my surprise, the colonel quietly told me to sit down. Naturally, I did so – although it seemed irregular to be sitting in front of a senior officer. He said, 'The censor's passed me a letter for you. It's from a vicar in London.' My mind reeled. The whole set-up seemed unreal and I wondered what on earth he was talking about. He continued, 'I'm very sorry to say that the letter contains some very sad news. The vicar says that some of his parishioners were killed in a recent Zeppelin raid and that they included your fiancée, Helen. Our chaplain recommends that I grant you compassionate leave and allow you time to grieve. If you request it, I'll grant you leave for the funeral and a few days beyond.'

"I left the room in a daze, only just remembering to thank and salute my CO. I went to see the padre and then made the biggest mistake of my life: I refused to take any leave. If I had only followed the padre's advice I might not still be grieving for her, twenty years after she died. But I thought my place was in the front line. What had been a duty had become a mission. I was determined to kill as many Germans as possible in revenge. The only good Germans were dead ones. Olga, I'm very sorry I thought that. Please forgive me."

"I think I can understand that, I feel it about the Nazis who caused me to lose the people that were dear to me. I'm very sorry about your fiancée."

He groaned. "That's part of the reason I've not told anyone before. I don't want pity. Of course I weep for her and wish she had not gone, but I also rejoice that we knew and loved each other – even if it was only for such a short time. I've shown you the photo because I want you to make a copy of it. It's too precious to take to away with me, but I do want her picture to remain beside my bed. Having seen what you've done with Noble and Magic, I know I can trust you to do Helen justice."

Olga tried to think of suitable words to accept, but Sam did not give her time to say anything.

"In addition to the skill you have shown, there's another reason that I want it to be you who does it …" There was a nervous pause. "Olga, you remind me of Helen. Obviously, your colouring is different, but your face and figure are very similar. Above all, your ears remind me of hers. They are, of course, not quite so delicate but they are the second most beautiful pair I've ever seen in my life."

If Sam had made a move at that moment, Olga knew she would have found him difficult to resist. In fact, she felt an urge to make the first move herself. But something stopped her from doing anything and the moment passed.

Over the next few weeks, Olga continued to enjoy her riding lessons and the tea afterwards in what she came to know as the Queen Anne room. Work continued on reproducing the photo. She made a point of not showing Samuel how she was getting on. By the time she felt that there was no more she could do to improve it, she had come to regard Helen as an old friend. When she gave Samuel the finished drawing, he kissed it gently.

"Thank you, my dear. I'll always treasure this. I won't insult you by offering to pay for

201

it but I'd like to give you a gift as a thank you." He produced a small package from his pocket and gave it to her. She opened it and found the diamond earrings inside.

"I can't possibly accept these!"

"I'll be leaving in a few days' time. Think of it as a farewell, a memento."

"They're far too precious; they mean so much to you."

"They've lain idle and useless in a box in a drawer for twenty years. I can't imagine anyone they'd suit better or who would appreciate them more. I think it's what Helen would want."

Olga could not speak as Samuel gently clipped the earrings to her delicate ears.

***

The Quakers did little to mark Christmas because, in theory, the nativity was celebrated every day – but Olga noted that the practice did not always live up to the theory. They did behave like everyone else in one respect – they gathered round their wireless for the king's speech. In a way it was a painful experience: people throughout the Empire willed him not to stutter but listened in rapt attention. The content of the king's broadcast was specifically Christian. He said Christmas was, "above all, the festival of peace."

"I believe from my heart," he said, "that the cause which binds together my peoples and our gallant and faithful Allies is the cause of Christian civilisation." Many would remember his final words for the rest of their lives.

> *I said to the man who stood at the Gate of the Year,*
>
> *"Give me a light that I may tread safely into the unknown."*
>
> *And he replied, "Go out into the darkness, and put your hand into the hand of God.*
>
> *That shall be to you better than light, and safer than a known way."*
>
> *May that Almighty Hand guide and uphold us all.*

A Child of Cologne

21

The Southolt Commonwealth

D unkirk was a defeat. However, thanks to the courage and fortitude of thousands of Royal Navy and civilian sailors, it was not the overwhelming disaster it might have been. The Royal Engineers played a vital role in blowing up bridges behind the lines and a thin grey line of tanks and men bravely delayed the enemy advance. Major Samuel Browne was amongst the tank commanders and Southolt waited anxiously to hear what had happened to him – but there was no news.

At last, a telegram from the War Office arrived at the hall. He was 'missing'.

William immediately summoned the staff and told them the news. At his suggestion, they kept silence for a quarter of an hour, thinking of 'the boss'. He then went through the instructions the major had left for this kind of situation. "Bert Simkins and Tom Yeoman will continue to be in charge of day-to-day matters in the hall and on the farm. I'll want a weekly report from each of you but won't interfere unless there's a problem. Are there any questions?"

Bert rose to his feet. "I've worked for the major for ten years and have great respect for him. I only hope to God he's still alive and will come home. My guess is that he is a prisoner of war and that it will be years rather than months before he's back here. I don't want to spend the war working for a conchie on something that does not help the war effort. Tomorrow, I'm going into Rowell to find a job in a munitions factory – and I advise the rest of you to do the same!" He walked out and others started to follow him.

"Hang on a minute, lads," said Tom as he got to his feet. "I understand how Bert feels, but what we're doing on the farm matters. Feeding everyone is vital, just as important as fighting, so I hope that none of the farm workers will leave. How sad it would be if the major comes back to a ruined farm with no animals. We owe it to him to keep things going. In any case, I like Mr Rowan, even though he's a conchie." Most of the farm workers sheepishly sat down again.

"Today was like Dunkirk," William said to Betty and Olga that evening. "We avoided disaster but not without heavy losses. Bert Simkins and his team have handed in their notice. Whether that is a good or bad thing only time will tell. I've no idea what they did with their time anyway so I'd planned to put the hall in mothballs for the moment. At least their decision has removed the problems of finding something for them to do and the cost of their pay. It's more worrying that we lost two of the farm hands. That's quite a lot on such a small farm. Not sure what we can do about that yet."

Olga and Betty chorused, "We can help!"

And that is how they came to learn how to milk a cow.

***

A couple of days later William discovered another problem. Over dinner he told Betty and Olga "I've been going through the books today and found, to my horror, that the insurance hasn't been paid. I don't know

207

whether Sam just forgot or if he thought Bert or I would deal with it. I phoned his insurers up and they said that, in the circumstances, they'd need to send an assessor round before they could renew."

It was weeks before the assessor came. He said he would need a certificate from someone like Rentokil to say the hall was sound. Getting a report from the Rentokil agent took weeks more and he did not bear good news.

"I'm very sorry to have to tell you that the hall is heavily infested with dry rot that will get much worse if action is not taken soon. Some of the ceilings will come down if the damage is not repaired. Here's our estimate of what it will cost to get rid of it."

William opened the envelope immediately and blanched. He decided that this was not a time for confidentiality and shared the problem. "There's not enough money to cover Rentokil's treatment, let alone the repairs. I could try to get a mortgage, but no bank will lend us anything. I don't think Sam has any friends who would be willing to bail us out. Amelia Stubbs is probably rich enough but they say she's tight-fisted. She'd only lend the money if she knew she'd get Sam himself as a reward."

"Now who's being un-Quakerly?"

"Sorry, Betty."

The trio fell into an unplanned, silent prayer.

After a while, thoughts bubbled up to the surface of Olga's mind. Thoughts she found difficult to articulate. They were too outlandish. Too absurd. But she could suppress them no longer. Automatically, she stood up to speak.

"I think we should start a community at the hall. There's space for plenty of people to live there. They could contribute money, skills or labour. There must be pacifists and socialists who have money they'd be willing to put in. You know several people who've been dismissed from their jobs and can't get work because they're conscientious objectors. They might be glad to use their skills or strength for the building work that would be needed … Sorry. I know it's a crazy idea … but I had to say it."

"Thank you, Olga," said William. "I don't think your idea is crazy. Wild, maybe. But not crazy. I'm not sure what Sam would think about it, but he's left me in charge and

I'm responsible for protecting his property – and the nation's heritage. If we did it, anyone who puts money in would have to be told that they wouldn't get it back. It would be impossible to unscramble the finances when Sam returns. On the other hand, they'd be guaranteed a roof over their heads until then. I had thought about contacting wealthy Quakers for help but there are fewer of them than there were a generation ago and their money is likely to be tied up in worthy causes. This is a much better idea."

"Could we not try both?"

"I'd rather not, dear. The wealthy benefactors might be tempted to interfere. I'd rather the community was a self-governing common-wealth."

The word came out of nowhere and remained out. To Betty and William it had echoes of the Diggers from the time of Cromwell and Fox and also of William Penn'

***

Betty took charge of the advertising. It was difficult to strike a balance between attempting to attract the right sort of people and not wanting to be prescriptive. When she felt that they were right. She showed them to William and Olga and after their approval sent them out to the Cadbury-owned *News Chronicle*, the *Manchester Guardian* and *The Friend*:

THE SOUTHOLT COMMONWEALTH

Applications are invited from tolerant people with the necessary talents (in the biblical or the modern sense of the word) to form a community in the pretty Suffolk village of Southolt.

The main task of the community will be to care for and repair Southolt Hall, an ancient manor house owned by a prisoner of war, which is suffering from a severe attack of dry rot.

Please send details of yourself and the gifts you can offer to: William Rowan, Apple Cottage, 15, Blossom Lane, Southolt, Suffolk; marking your envelope 'The Southolt Commonwealth'.

At breakfast time on the Monday morning after the adverts had gone out, there was a knock on the door of Apple Cottage. It was

Tom Yeoman, looking worried and unwell. Betty gave him a cup of tea straight away.

"I'm afraid I've some bad news," he said, and hesitated before continuing. "Both the remaining farm hands handed in their notice when they saw the advert. They'll be leaving at the end of the month."

William's face paled. "I'm sorry. I've made a blunder; I should have consulted you all before the advert went out, even though the change doesn't affect the farm directly. I do hope *you're* not thinking of leaving." Tom gave a grunt which William found reassuring but Betty did not and he still looked troubled.

"Is there something you're not telling us? What is it?"

"It's my wife, Molly. For a number of weeks she's been going to the dance hall in Liffham on Saturday nights and not getting home till after midnight. The RAF NCOs go there because it's so far from their base that they don't have to compete with the pilots and other officers. I can't say that I am happy about it because she is my wife and if I'm honest, I'm jealous, but it makes her so happy and I love to see that. I only wish that she felt like that because of something I have done. I don't dance and don't want to learn so I can't go with her. It is making me feel wretched. What can I do?"

Olga sensed that her two friends were about to give conflicting advice and so she rushed to speak first. "I think this is something William and Betty will need time to sleep on and to think and pray about. Would it be all right if they talked to you later?"

Reluctantly he agreed.

Olga couldn't help worrying about the situation while she washed up – even though she knew it was not really her problem. As well as the animals Sam had shown her on her first visit, there was a small herd of Jacob sheep. Then there was the ten-acre field, the large kitchen garden and the apple orchard. Tom would need help from the newcomers as well as William, Betty and herself to cope with it all. The trouble was that they had no idea what knowledge, experience and ability those people would have. She was just about to start her letter to her father when there was another knock on the door. She opened it and saw a man in the habit of a Benedictine monk. Before she could recover from her surprise he spoke.

"Please, excuse me. I'm Brother Karl and I'm looking for the Southolt community."

"You've come to the right place, but William and Betty Rowan are out for the rest of the afternoon. Meanwhile, you're very welcome to come in and wait. My name is Olga Muller. Would you like a cup of tea?"

"Yes, please. Am I right in assuming from your name that you're German?"

"Yes, I had to escape from Cologne with the Kindertransport because I had an African grandmother. Had because Nazis murdered her on Kristallnacht."

After a pause, she asked him if he was German too.

Brother Karl confirmed her supposition and tried to continue the conversation in German, but their dialects were too far apart for it to be easy and they reverted to English. "I came to England in 1930. I was disturbed at the way things were going then, but I'd no idea that they would move so far or so fast. So, I came not to escape but to work and to help repay, in part, the debt that the Church in Germany owes to England – the school I went to was called Saint Boniface, so I was aware of his mission from an early age. You as a German will know what I am talking

214

about but I have been astonished how few English people know the part that he played in converting the German tribes. When I heard that my order was looking for volunteers to build – or rather, rebuild – a monastery church in his county of Devonshire I jumped at the opportunity. There was a small group of us, all German, and I was very happy although the work was hard. That is, I was very happy until the work on the church was complete last year.

"The abbey makes a potent tonic wine that's very popular with the tourists who've come to visit over the last few years and, I regret to say, with me. The abbot allowed us to drink a certain amount but one week I exhausted my ration early and stole a bottle from the shop. The theft was noticed and I confessed. The abbot forgave me and urged me to ensure there was no repetition. Unfortunately, my addiction was too strong and I broke the rules again.

"By then, war had broken out. We were given seven days to sign an agreement saying we would not to leave the abbey grounds. If we refused, we would be interred for the duration. Not surprisingly, my fellow monks agreed to sign. I wrote a farewell note regretting my continued failure and thanking the community for their friendship. I put it in a prominent place and left in the middle of the night. By a quirk of fate, I met the abbot as I went. He did not show any surprise, and just gave me a blessing.

"I've spent the time since working on farms or buildings in exchange for bed and food. I've always made a point of saying that I'm a German and why I'm in England and, generally, I've been welcomed and accepted. Successive employers have been delighted to get hardworking help so cheaply. I worked my way east across the south of England, and then through the Home Counties towards East Anglia. I've had no plan until recently, I decided to visit the shrine of Our Lady of Walsingham to recharge my spiritual batteries. However I saw your advert and instantly knew that this is where God wants me to be and that's why I'm here today."

Brother Karl asked if he could see the hall, so Olga took him to the ancient building and gave him a quick tour. They spent most time in the parts where the dry rot was worst but she was delighted show him the chapel. It had been deconsecrated years before but it still had a distinct aura. The ornate Italianate altar remained, flanked by stained-glass windows of saints. Although the nineteenth century had hardly been the best period for stained glass, these had a certain charm. Olga pointed out a small window high in the west wall but did not explain what was significant about it until they went upstairs. She opened a door and showed the monk a small, plain room with a little window at one end. When he looked through it he was taken aback to see the inside of the chapel.

"Even now, this is known as the nuns' sickroom. Would you like it as your bedroom?"

Karl was astounded that this youngster seemed to have been given so much authority, but accepted with alacrity.

As it happened, the youngster herself was astounded by what she had just done and wondered what Betty and even more, William, would have to say.

***

Later that evening when Karl had gone to his room William turned to Olga.

"Whatever got into you? How could you offer a room to someone neither Betty nor I had ever met?"

Olga could not think of a reply and stood in silence while William continued.

"Nevertheless, I think it's a brilliant idea. No family would want that room. It's unattractive and its name is even worse. On the other hand, it could almost have been made for Karl. Well done."

So, after a tumultuous day, Olga went to bed happy.

"I'm glad Olga did it," Betty said to William. "It shows that she's an adult and a sensible member of our family."

***

Tom once again came knocking on the cottage door at breakfast time on the following Monday. This time, he looked even grimmer and less well. After he had sat down Olga made him a cup of tea. Having drunk the tea he regained some of his composure and started his story.

"On Saturday night, the same NCO rode up to my house on a motorbike. I was surprised and went out to speak to him. I'd hardly opened my mouth when Molly swept out, dressed up to the nines, jumped onto the pillion seat and they roared off. At half past three in the morning, the police came knocking on my door. He had tried to overtake a Bentley on a blind corner and crashed headlong into a lorry. He and Molly died instantly. When the police had gone, I ran out of the cottage shouting and swearing. I've not been back since – I've spent most of my time in the barn at the hall with the rats and cats. I hope that's all right with you?"

Betty went to Tom and put her arms around him. "Oh Tom how awful, I am so sorry. Of course it's all right. You must move into the hall, you should not be sleeping in the barn. Please, choose yourself a nice room or rooms there and we'll arrange for whatever you want from your cottage to be moved there."

Tom nodded "You are kind."

"Let us know if there is anything that we can do, anything at all," said William who was clearly shaken.

Tom got up, walked over to William and shook his hand. "Thank you, thank you, thank you," he said quietly.

***

Applications had come in slowly but steadily. The Rowans were disappointed that none had come from Quakers. The family quickly agreed that the choices could not be made on the strength of the letters alone so almost everyone was sent further particulars and invited to an interview. The only exception was a sixteen-year old boy who had nothing to offer the community as he had no skills or money. In his application he said that he wanted to leave home and thought that his parents would be more accepting and not try to entice him back if he was part of a community. While sympathetic the Rowans were acutely aware of the possibility of adverse publicity when his parents found out where he was.

After the interviews, the applications were put into three piles: yes, no and maybe. There were only two applications in each of the last two piles. An evangelical Christian who used the interview as an opportunity to attempt to 'save' them was out, as was a foul-mouthed Marxist whose only subject of conversation was the class war.

A Child of Cologne

There were two pairs of maybes. One was a married woman and her lover; Betty and William liked the couple and were tolerant towards them but were concerned about the possible reaction in the village and worried about what the popular press would do if their story became known. Olga was very hesitant, knowing only too well what Father Michael's attitude would be. For better or for worse, they decided that there were probably enough without them and so they were added to the no pile. The other pair, had frankly admitted in their application that they were homosexuals. As the interview progressed, it became clear that they were a couple and were hoping that the community would be a place where they could express their love in safety. As a lawyer, William knew that this would put members of the community in danger of being charged as accessories and he said he would not expose others to this risk.

That left eleven adults and six children in the yes pile. Including the Rowans – who had put their cottage on the market, Tom and Karl, the new commonwealth consisted of fifteen adults, six children – and Olga, who could not properly be described as either.

Everyone was invited to gather in the hall at half eleven on Saturday October 19th.

At ten, Olga and Karl were stationed in the cottage overlooking the farmyard gate that was the main entrance to the grounds. They were on the lookout for the newcomers and, twenty minutes later, the bus from Manningtree station dropped the first ones off.

Karl opened the gate and led them into the cottage where Olga welcomed them, introducing herself as the Rowans' daughter and offering tea.

Reginald Bytheway was surprised to be greeted by two Germans, which seemed odd to him over a year after the start of the war, but he did not comment on it. He simply accepted the offer of tea, and introduced his wife, Geraldine, and their daughters. "Avril is twelve and we are assuming that she will be able to go to Rowell Grammar School. Julie is only ten so she will be at the local school for the time being but we hope and expect that she will pass the eleven plus and join Avril."

Olga took them on a short tour of the hall and left them with Betty and William in the Queen Anne room. When she got back to the cottage, she found Karl deep in conversation with Frank and Gladys Morgan.

Karl introduced Olga to them and their eight-year-old daughter Gill and said, "Frank may be a Methodist preacher but, like me, he has a deep reverence for both the Virgin Mary and for Saint Francis of Assisi."

Frank corrected him, pointing out that, while he revered Mary as the mother of Jesus, he was not at all sure she was a virgin.

"I'm a Roman Catholic, too," said Olga, "so you can guess what I believe about her. But there'll be plenty of time to discuss it later. I can see another car at the gate, so I need to take you on a whirlwind tour of the hall while Karl gets them some tea." As she started this second tour, she couldn't help thinking that the simple plan that had seemed so sensible at breakfast time was, when put into practice, one that involved more rapid rushing in and out through doors than a West End farce.

The car she had seen pulling up had contained Alan and Cynthia Stevens. Their five-year-old daughter had introduced herself as Elizabeth before monopolising the conversation. Only Olga's return stopped her and created a lull in which Geoffrey Steele could introduce himself, his wife Margaret and their eleven-year-old son, David. They had left their three-year-old daughter, Dorothy, at home in West Bromwich with her grandparents. Olga decided it would be more practical to take the two families around the hall together.

James Green did not arrive until quarter past twelve, his guitar strapped to his back. He apologised for being so late, explaining that his car had suffered a puncture near Whipsnade. He amused them with his anecdote about the camel in the field next to where he'd stopped to change the wheel: it had stood there chewing and looking down its nose at him.

They knew Dick Shepherd would be late. He was an Anglican pacifist training to be a chartered accountant in Colchester. His employers allowed him one Saturday morning off each month, and this was not one of those. He arrived on his motorbike at ten to one and immediately joined everyone else in the Queen Anne dining room.

This was William's signal. He rose to his feet and the conversation subsided. He announced that the remaining member of the community, Oswald Winters, had phoned that morning to send apologies, he would not be able to make it that day. He had not explained why in detail, just said he was having "a spot of bother".

It was a lovely warm day, so William's suggestion that they should take lunch outside was greeted with cheers. William asked everyone to speak about themselves for a few moments during lunch as a way of introducing themselves to the others. Everyone was soon chatting happily and enjoying the picnic under a clear blue sky. But then their conversation was interrupted.

"I'm bored! I want to go home!" shouted Elizabeth. When no one reacted to this outcry immediately, she marched up to the weed-covered pond beside the lawn and threw Ming, her cuddly toy panda cub, into the water. Alan rolled his trousers up to the knees, waded in and rescued it.

As lunch drew to a close, William asked Tom to tell everyone about the farm and the jobs that need to be done to run it. He then gave every family a plan of the building, explaining that it had been divided into units, each bearing the name of a famous author. The families were asked to show on their plans which unit they would prefer to live in, and to rate their top three preferences. William also asked everyone to work out what help they could give with the farm, and to again list their preferences in order. He suggested that the new arrivals spent some time exploring the building in more detail to help them decide before returning for a formal meeting at half past three. By general consensus, this too would take place on the lawn.

The mothers asked Olga if she would be willing to look after their offspring during the meeting. Olga hesitated. The prospect of trying to control Elizabeth filled her with foreboding. However, she could see no practical alternative and agreed to do it. They suggested she take the children to the village shop for sweets and comics, entrusting her with the necessary money and the even more valuable ration books. Elizabeth chose dolly mixtures and the *Mickey Mouse* comic, the sisters chose a large box of liquorice allsorts and *The Dandy* and *Wizard* to share. David had decided not to go on the trip but had asked Olga to buy him a block of Cadbury's dark chocolate which he would share with her. He explained that he had Arthur Mee's *Children's Newspaper* each week and, when the other children were not listening, said that he thought comics were really rather silly.

David did not go with his parents on their tour, but sought out Karl instead. "I found what you said when we were introducing ourselves very interesting. I spent the second part of August last year with my aunt and uncle who have a guest house in Buckfastleigh. Mum put me on the train at Snow Hill, Birmingham and asked the guard to keep an eye on me until we reached Newton Abbot where my aunt would meet me. I was a bit puzzled but not frightened. I thought of the journey as an adventure. My stay with my aunt was boring but not, on the whole, unpleasant. The thing I enjoyed most was my visit the abbey with my cousin Fred who runs a Scout troop there. One of the monks led us onto the abbey roof, which Fred told me was a rare privilege. The view of the village, the River Dart and the countryside beyond was breathtaking."

"I know! I was the monk that took you onto the roof. I remember your face was open-eyed with wonder. However, the abbey was buzzing with rumours about you a few days later: something to do with the

Ashburton crossroads. What exactly happened?"

"It was really boring at the guest house. My aunt was extremely busy and could spare little time for me. Even Fred had other interests which kept him busy most of the time. There was a garden to play in, but it was very small. The only bit of excitement was a mound next to the wall at one end that I could climb to watch the cars go by on the Exeter to Land's End Road. In the middle of the wall was a gate. I hadn't been told not to go out of it. Maybe my aunt thought that it was obvious. One day I went out and started walking up the road. After a while I came to the Ashburton crossroads. We lived near major crossroads at home but they always had traffic lights or a policeman at them. I was horrified to see that this one had neither so I took charge of the situation: I went to the middle of the crossroad and directed the traffic as I had seen policemen do. Sometime later, my aunt arrived on the scene, looking worried and angry. Nothing much was said but I knew I was in trouble. A couple of days later, my mother came and took me home.

"It was only a week later that I was evacuated to Tamworth with the rest of my school. It was not a great surprise because, while I was at the guesthouse, I had sat alone in the lounge and listened to the wireless announcer reading out a long list of the towns from which children were to be evacuated if war broke out. West Bromwich starts with a W so I to wait what seemed a long time to hear it named. I had known all along that it was bound to be included but, nevertheless, it felt odd when I heard it. It did not seem real. West Bromwich was never mentioned on the wireless without the addition of the word 'Albion'. By Christmas, it was decided that it was safe for us to go back home and stay there."

Yes. That's the story I heard – except, of course, for the bit about the broadcast. What you don't appear to know is that your mother had agreed that you could stay in Devon with your aunt if and when war broke out. But after the crossroads incident, your uncle said that you would remain over his dead body, and that's why your mother had to come and fetch you."

"Thank you. That makes sense. I should've known Mum was doing her best for me all along."

Olga led her party back through the churchyard instead of along the street. She pointed out the belfry, proud to be able to explain that it had never been completed because the Suffolk-born Cardinal Wolsey had fallen from favour with Henry VIII while he had been financing it. For the past four hundred years, the bells had been housed in a wooden shed without side walls in the churchyard. The bell ringers were the only people allowed in, and they had to wear special earmuffs to protect them from the intense noise. Olga told the children how, before the war, she enjoyed watching the ringers at work, summoning people for weddings, funerals and Sunday services. But the bells had been silent for the past year, and everyone feared hearing them now. Their sound would signal that the Nazis had invaded. Olga dreaded the prospect. She felt no hope of being able to escape them a second time.

***

William called the afternoon meeting to order explaining that, for now, Betty would chair and he would act as secretary so that

they could get off to a quick start. They
would hold annual general meetings and he
hoped that by the time of the next they would
know one another well enough to make
informed choices about their successors. In
the meantime, they would need someone to
be an honorary finance officer and look after
the bank accounts that had been set up with
Barclays: one for the building, another for the
farm and a third for the household. Someone
nominated Dick Shepherd as treasurer
because of his accountancy skills. He
reluctantly agreed. Each of these actions was
ratified by a formal resolution.

They moved on to more contentious
issues. Betty asked for these to be settled after
the manner of Quakers: in other words, as if
a family meeting rather than a company one.
There would rarely, if ever, be votes but each
individual would have the power to veto a
proposal – although they would be expected
to use this privilege sparingly. After a lot of
haggling, they agreed to share each month's
household costs pro rata with children
counting as half. The farm would sell food to
the household, charging double the base cost
to take account of labour and incidentals.
They set up rotas for cooking, washing-up,

shopping and cleaning common areas. Some people proposed sanctions for those who failed to do their turn, but none seemed particularly practical so, in the end, all they could agree on was to rely on peer pressure – even though almost everyone thought that this was a cop-out. A more pleasant decision was to invite the villagers to an opening party.

The meeting was interrupted by a tremendous noise. A Hurricane flew low over them, a German fighter hot on its heels. Everyone held their breath. But, at the last possible moment, the British fighter banked steeply upwards, looped the loop and came down on the tail of the Jerry with all guns blazing. The assembled pacifists and neo-pacifists broke into a cheer as the enemy plane caught fire. But the cheer was short lived, dying out as they realised that no parachute had emerged from the carnage. However wrong his ideas, they acknowledged that a brave young man had died a terrible premature death.

A subdued and sombre group resumed the meeting.

***

Olga had decided to keep the children out of the way by leading them on an expedition round the building. She took them past the downstairs WC, having checked that none of them needed to use it, and climbed the central stairs. The younger ones explored the upstairs part of the north wing while she listened, fascinated, to David who had joined her and was excitedly describing his conversation with Karl. Soon the children gathered around them and she realised that one was missing. With a sense of alarm she interrupted him.

"Where's Elizabeth?"

She split the remaining children into parties to scour the place shouting the girl's name. They had no success. Olga realised that she had to face the music and tell the adults.

As she passed the downstairs WC on her way out, she heard muffled screams. Elizabeth had locked herself in and could not open the door from the inside. David went off to get help from the adults while the girls stayed to reassure Elizabeth.

Karl was the first grown-up to arrive. As soon as he knew what the problem was, he asked if anyone had a penknife. David produced one and Karl chipped away the putty surrounding the window and then gently took out the glass. He was just about to climb in when Olga stopped him.

"I'm a little slimmer than you and, in any case, I feel sort of responsible."

Karl looked down at his beer belly and had to agree.

After her parents had comforted Elizabeth, Alan stood up and said, "Cynthia and I have talked it over and agree that this is the last straw. We're going to gather our things together and head home. We wish you all well but don't see how the community can survive for long when it's so badly organised."

A few minutes later, their car drove past the lawn and on to the road. Alan tooted the horn, and the Southolt Commonwealth raised an ironic cheer of relief.

22

The Commonwealth's Early Days

"Careless Talk Costs Lives," the posters said. To many of the villagers who came to the party, this seemed a place where the warning might be particularly true. They stuck together in small clusters, avoiding their hosts as much as they could without being impolite, fearful in case the conchies heard them talking about the progress of the war. Their main topic of conversation, was the rumour of heavy losses from the raids on East Anglian airfields. The latest indications were that Hitler – and it could only be Hitler – had decided to bomb civilian targets instead.

"Thank God they are bombing London," said one visitor to another, "I know that's a terrible thing to say but I don't know what would happen otherwise."

On the other hand some of the villagers went out of their way to be welcoming to the

incomers – for a while at least. They joined in
the dancing on the lawn to the
accompaniment of Jimmy's guitar and
listened to the children singing folk songs.
They went home somewhat less frightened of
the monster that had entered their village.

The new residents of the hall moved in,
over the next few months. Between his legal
work and helping Tom, William was fully
occupied. Betty had her hands full too. She
was helping both William and Tom, clearing
out Apple Cottage and still had
responsibilities as treasurer of Rowell's
Quaker meeting. It therefore fell to Olga to
welcome people and help them get settled.
She found great delight in doing these things.
It made her feel important and useful and
gave her an opportunity to get to know the
newcomers better.

The community discussed problems and
made plans at regular Friday evening
meetings. A perennial item on early agendas
was the Morgans' cat: people were fed up
with clearing up the mess it left all over the
hall. Fortunately, it soon started to spend
more time out of doors and ceased to be
considered a problem once people
recognised the good job it was doing in

controlling the population of rats and mice. Remembering Agamemnon Olga had reservations about this but did not share them with anyone, even the Rowans.

The problems arising from the presence of children were more intractable. Each set of parents had different rules which led to confusion and resentment. Julie complained that Gill was allowed to stay up until eight even though she was younger. She was rather cross that this was permitted and felt that she should be the one staying up later as a perk of being older. Men who had stayed at the Red Lion longer than was perhaps wise complained about the noise the children made in the mornings. Women who had spent time painting the corridor walls complained about the children kicking balls indoors. Cooks who had to carry heavy saucepans of boiling water and hot food complained about the hazards caused by having children in the kitchen. That one was more serious so children were banned from the kitchen while meals were being prepared but the boys often forgot and some of the girls pestered to be allowed to "help".

The children themselves soon banded into mini gangs which each found a den of its own, and were soon reconciled after their frequent fallings out. Visiting relatives – even those who did not like or approve of other aspects life at the hall – would say how lovely a place it was for children to grow up in.

The parents, too, recognised how lucky their children were – and how lucky they were to have a dozen or so babysitters often available. However, they also recognised the danger: having everybody responsible could mean nobody would be responsible. One particular incident made this clear in a most striking way.

***

The hall's hens had not laid for a day or two so Betty went to the village shop to buy eggs. She drove in because she was going into Rowell afterwards, and left the car in the layby next to the church and opposite the hall. As she came back through the churchyard, she came across Julie eating yew berries. Betty knew they were poisonous and panicked. She did not know if there was an antidote. She had no idea where Julie's parents were. She could not even think of anyone else in the community who might know either of these things – or be able to help in any other way. She decided, for better or worse, to take Julie the ten miles to Rowell hospital's casualty ward. She had always been an even more careful driver than William but, on this occasion, she ignored such minor matters as speed limits.

She was about half way there when she heard a siren and saw flashing lights in her mirror. The police car drew up in front of her to force her to stop and Betty worried that the delay would prevent her getting to the hospital on time. But, once she had explained the situation, the constable put his book away and told her to follow him. He put his lights and siren on again and she managed to go even faster.

At the hospital, Betty gave as many details as she could, telling the nurse that she was a close neighbour and friend. When the nurse asked if the parents had a telephone she was relieved to be able to give the number for the communal one. Sometime later the nurse reported back that she had phoned several times but there was no answer. Betty was disappointed but not surprised for the phone sat in a room that, although central, was seldom used for anything other than outgoing calls.

Julie was discharged three hours later and the journey home was much calmer and quieter than the journey out – or, indeed, the reception they received on their return. A frantic Geraldine rushed out as the car drew in and demanded to know what Betty had been doing with her daughter all this time. All the strain and worry of the morning came flooding back and Betty did something she had rarely done before. She lost her temper.

"I've been saving her life and this is all the thanks I get for my efforts!"

Geraldine was embarrassed into silence.

"I'm sorry I didn't manage to send you a message. It must have been very worrying for you not knowing where she was, but my priority was to get her to hospital as soon as possible. I came across her eating yew berries in the churchyard."

Geraldine put her arms around Betty. "Please forgive me. I should have trusted you. I can't thank you enough for all you have done."

The community set up separate groups to manage the pigs, sheep, hens, cows and kitchen garden but these did not need formal meetings as problems were discussed while working. Tom was an ex-officio member of each group. Olga and Betty continued to do the milking with James, who had worked at Whipsnade, as backup. He also put his experience with animals to use caring for the pigs and sheep. Margaret had a special liking for pigs and so chose to work with them, while Geraldine gravitated to the sheep group because she was very fond of lambs. William liked to get his fingers dirty and so focussed on work on the land, but everyone else preferred variety and moved from group to group.

They discussed matters of long-term interest to the community on the first Sunday of each month. Everyone was expected to attend the all-day meetings – even if they had to travel some distance because they had not yet moved in. The agenda might include who should occupy which rooms and what financial contributions each family should make. Or what crops should be grown and where. Or the allocation of domestic duties. The latter was to prove a major cause of dissension. Some men found more important things to do at times they were allocated to cooking, shopping or washing-up. Even sleep might suddenly become necessary. The mothers would get very frustrated when they had to, yet again, produce meals from emergency supplies at short notice. Olga noticed that some men who were fond of making stands in favour of women's equality at meetings had principles that often evaporated in the heat of the kitchen.

By the end of March 1941 everyone was in and more or less settled. Work on both the farm and the building was in full swing and, despite many hold ups, progress was being made. Disagreements were common and aired at the Friday meetings. Betty would ask for a period of silence and the way forward would emerge often from this. But at the first meeting in May, silence was not enough.

Reginald's brother had been killed in an air raid that left the rest of the family homeless. Could they come and live at the hall? Everyone expressed sympathy but most people felt that it would be very difficult to fit them all in – and it would open the floodgates. Reginald threatened to raise the subject every week until the community changed its mind.

And then Germany invaded the Soviet Union. This changed everything for Oswald

Winters. He had viewed the war as a fight between two capitalist countries, but now he was eager to support the soviets against the fascists and announced that he was leaving the community to join the army. And so the problem of Reginald's in-laws – Florence and her son, Arnold – was resolved.

Oswald's departure solved another problem, one that had not been discussed. When he had encountered Olga or Betty alone, he had tried to touch them. Olga had used her favourite tactic; Betty had simply told him firmly and quietly to never try it again. Although they had both kept quiet, feeling no harm had been done, they were still embarrassed whenever they met him and so they were relieved to see him go.

***

One of the more popular duties was collecting the post from the village Post Office, and handing it out over breakfast. Olga's 'red-letter days' were few and far between she was always overjoyed to receive a letter from her father – even though he could say little more than that he was still alive and that he loved her very much. But then she got a letter which was not from her father. It was from his uncle, Father Josef.

Dearest Olga,

I'm very sad to report that your dear father died at 7:30 PM on 24 April. There was an air raid and he had a heart attack as we were going into the crypt. The other priests and I did our best to revive him. I administered extreme unction myself. He had been talking about you only minutes earlier.

The cathedral was crowded for his funeral. Many people brought in examples of his art and these were used to decorate the building: a worthy and fitting tribute to someone I think was a great artist and a great man – although some people might consider me a little prejudiced. I could not help remembering the little boy who stood beside me during his father's funeral and who has done so much more since.

He visited Gestapo headquarters every week to seek news of your mother but he was always rebuffed with harshness. You can imagine the kind of things he had to endure. I told him it was pointless, but he insisted on going,

*saying he had to persevere for her sake
and for yours. Sometimes, I was able to
go with him – although I dreaded doing
so. The place smells of the fear and death
and misery of the prisoners tortured
there (I can write of such matters
because, unlike your father's letters, this
one is being smuggled out via the
Vatican). I'm sure those visits were a
major cause of his heart problem.*

*I hope and pray that one day you and
I will be able to meet again and talk about
your dear father face to face.*

*All your friends in the cathedral send
their love and sympathy.*

Yours in God's love,
Father Josef

***

When the next batch of letters arrived Olga
felt a sadness as she knew that there could
not be anything for her, so she was surprised
when Betty passed her a letter. Her shriek on
reading it caused everyone to turn their
heads.

"Sam is alive and well and in a POW camp
somewhere in Bavaria," she explained. But
most people in the room just stared until she

added, "You know, Major Browne, who owns the hall." Then she realised with a sudden surprise that only she, William and Betty had ever met him even though his personality was all around. He had selected the pictures on the walls, many were of his own ancestors, together with photographs of his days at Harrow and the library was full of books he had chosen or inherited.

Olga re-read the letter with a mixture of pleasure and misgiving.

My dear Olga,

As you can see from the address above, I am a POW in Bavaria. Fortunately, I am well and was not injured in the fighting. Rumour has it that our rearguard action was invaluable in helping so many escape from Dunkirk and elsewhere. This thought gives me great consolation as I gaze on this dreary camp and eat its dreadful food. Bavaria is supposed to be a lovely part of the world but this place is anything but. Nothing but greyness.

One thing that brings brightness to my days is taking out the pictures of Helen, Magic and Noble and feasting my eyes on them. Something else that cheers me up is the picture of your face, especially your ears, in my mind's eye. I hope you wear the earrings from time to time and think about me a little.

I am only allowed one letter a week and this is my first. Please let Betty and William and everyone else know that I am alive and well. Could you also, please, make a special point of letting Lady Stubbs know that I will be writing to her next week?

There were indecipherable crossings out, before he signed off with 'Your good friend, Sam.'

"Be careful, my dear," said Betty when Olga showed her the letter. "Love can have very long arms. I feel very angry that he should have asked you, of all people, to go to see Amelia Stubbs. I'll go with you, I'm not frightened of that woman."

"Thank you for your offer, but this is a visit I feel I have to undertake alone. I'll tell you when I go so I know your thoughts are with me – and so you can call out the police if I've not returned within twenty-four hours!"

Olga walked the four miles to Stratford
Saint Mary and knocked on the great door of
Stubbs Hall. The butler answered the door.

"Her Ladyship is not at home," he said.

Olga knew he was lying so she went for a
walk in the grounds and visited the horses in
the paddock and, half an hour later, she
knocked again. This produced the same
result, but she kept trying intermittently for a
couple of hours. Eventually, the butler gave
in and Olga was ushered into the presence of
Amelia Stubbs.

"Why on earth are you bothering me? I
cannot imagine that we have anything to say
to each other."

"Sam is alive and well in a POW camp and
has asked me to let you know."

The smile that spread across Lady Stubbs'
face at first was so bright that it was almost
beautiful, but it was quickly replaced by a
look of unbridled hatred and fury.

"Why would he want to communicate
with me through a nobody like you? A
German nobody at that?"

"I don't know. But I do know he cared
enough to specifically ask me to visit you."

Lady Stubbs stood in front of Olga in
silence for a while before apologising. "I'm

sorry. It must have taken courage to come to me with that message. I think Sam was most unreasonable to put a youngster like you through such an ordeal. Please stay and have some tea."

When Olga took the news around the village it was greeted with pleasure, but there were many raised eyebrows as people wondered why the major had entrusted his message to a pretty young foreigner.

***

The community felt that Christmas 1941 should be a time for festivities, despite the war and rationing. The children had smaller presents than in earlier years but they seemed to accept it. They put on a pantomime, *Cinderella*. Jimmy wrote the script and songs, Avril and David were the leads, Olga was pleased to play one of the mice who drew the coach and Betty was flattered to be asked to be the fairy godmother. Because most of the humour consisted of in-jokes, it was decided at a Friday meeting not to invite villagers and so the cast outnumbered the spectators. The land group chopped down a large fir tree they had found on the farm and brought it into the Queen Anne room. The children covered it with decorations they had made themselves.

On Christmas Day, while they were eating the home-reared geese, Dorothy asked what fir trees had to do with Christmas. Margaret started to tell her how Prince Albert, the husband of Queen Victoria, had first brought them to England. But Karl, who was sitting nearby, stood up and repeated the question and answer for the benefit of those sitting further away.

"But," he said, "very few English people know the full story and that, I think, is a pity. Back in the seventh century, an Anglo-Saxon monk, Saint Boniface, came from south-west England to convert the heathen German tribes. They were led by Druids and worshipped under sacred oak trees. Saint Boniface looked for a powerful symbol of the Trinity to compete with the oak and chose the fir tree. As you'll have gathered, the saint and his tree triumphed and Germany became Christian. Whether you can say Germany is Christian today is debatable but I'd like to ask you for a two-minute silence to pray for the spirit of Saint Boniface to return there."

***

As the days went by Olga found herself worrying about what had become of her mother now that her father's letter no longer came. Slowly she came to accept that she would never see either of her beloved parents again. To some extent their place was taken by Betty and William who treated her like a daughter. Sam wrote to her once a month and to Amelia during the other weeks. A friendship grew between the two women and she went over to Stubbs Hall weekly to either share her letter with Amelia or to hear what Sam had written. Their mutual love was the horses and Olga enjoyed going for a hack with her new companion.

***

Betty's birthday was on the last day of May. Olga had little money for a present but got up early intending to boil an egg so she could take Betty breakfast in bed. She went to the kitchen, found the timer and put the kettle on. As she turned on the radio, the announcer was reporting on the latest RAF action.

"In the early hours of this morning, Bomber Command reported the success of Operation Millennium, the first thousand-bomber raid. The target was the city of Cologne. Forty of our aircraft failed to return."

The egg was never boiled.

Betty came downstairs to find a kitchen full of steam and Olga crumpled in a heap on the floor.

23
30–31 May 1942

Hans was at an airfield near Koblenz, when he received the letter from Frieda.

My dear Hans,

Great news! My baby daughter was born yesterday. I have named her Sophia and she is both very well and very beautiful. I'm tired but the nuns say that I'm doing well. They don't say that I'm very beautiful. Surprise, surprise!

I've not told Mother and Father. They have never been to visit me and I don't want them to. I know that if they do they will only resume their campaign for me to acknowledge one of the Hermans as the father and then pretend it is a wonderful thing. I'll never do that, and I can only hope that they have now got the message.

It would be a great sin to describe my other piece of news as "good" but I can't resist rejoicing in the knowledge that both the Hermans are now lying dead in a Russian field. My flesh still creeps at what they did to me., The way I feel at the moment it is very doubtful that I'll ever marry any man.

My baby is a delightful joy, and I am so very grateful that I didn't have an abortion. I know very well that you advised it with my best interests at heart – and I love you for that – but you were wrong, quite mistaken.

Please come and see us as soon as possible.

Your loving sister,
Frieda

Hans tore the letter up into little pieces, thankful that no one else had seen it and thinking that, for once, Frieda had not been very wise.

He secured a forty-eight-hour pass and went to the railway station – only to be told that all trains to Cologne had been cancelled for the next two days due to enemy action.

Hans was in a quandary. It was little use trying to hitch a lift by road because there were very few civilian cars around. Then he had a brilliant idea. He remembered that the Rhine barges went through Cologne. He wandered down to the docks where the large barges stopped. He was in luck, there was one in so he jumped on board.

A burly, sunburnt man came up and, seeing the Luftwaffe uniform, welcomed him saying. "I'm Konrad Schweizer. Any member of our brave air force is welcome on my barge. What can I do for you?"

Hans told him the situation but missed out certain irrelevant facts about Frieda.

"I'll be sailing at six but I must warn you that I will not be stopping at Cologne itself but about five kilometres beyond. I have a girl-friend there and will be able to stay with her for a couple of hours in the middle of the night without anyone knowing. You should be able to walk back to the city quite easily from there."

Hans was suitably grateful and returned in plenty of time. He quickly found a comfortable place to lie using his backpack as a pillow. The gentle motion of the boat would probably have lulled him to sleep were it not for the glorious sunset straight ahead. It looked as if the river was swallowing the sun and sending freshly mined pots of Rheingold to the surface. As the sun disappeared, the stars came out one by one and filled the cloudless sky. Thanks to his training, he knew many of them by name. Konrad came over and chatted from time to time although it was not safe for him to leave the steering wheel for very long. He, too, was fascinated by the stars.

They had been floating pleasantly downstream for about three hours when Hans became vaguely aware of a change in the distant sky. The stars seemed to be vanishing and then re-appearing. He got to his feet and wandered down to the wheelhouse to ask Konrad about it.

"There's going to be a big one tonight."

"A big what?"

"Why, air raid, of course! The stars are being obscured by enemy aircraft – and there are a lot of them. God help Cologne – and God help your sister!"

They could hear the distant sound of anti-aircraft guns. Bombs were exploding. Searchlights lit up the sky. Two beams crossed, catching a Lancaster. They watched as a shell blew up the bomber. Konrad cheered and led Hans on a dance around the deck.

Hans' feelings were ambivalent. He knew there were people on that plane, people who had died. On the other hand, a much larger number of German civilians would probably have been killed had it not been destroyed. But he must not show Konrad any sign of his doubts, the struggles beneath the surface.

As they travelled the sky ahead grew redder and redder and then orange. The noise of the bombs and planes increased to a deafening roar. Hans looked back upstream and saw the bombers wheel round in tight formation so they could make their way home by another route. There were gaps in the squadrons but Hans knew that these were not enough to deter them from coming back another day. The raid continued. He could see the cathedral's twin spires silhouetted against the angry fires. On the outskirts of the city the damage was relatively light, but it was worse towards the centre. Soon there were no undamaged buildings to be seen – and few people to be seen either. Ambulances and fire engines appeared through the smoke from time to time but were eerily silent. Karl kept to the west side of the river, the one further from the worst of the bombing but still the heat and the smoke were intense as they went through the centre of the city. For a while the intensity slowly, very slowly, subsided. Then a new smell hit him. It was worse than that from the sulphurous smoke but he did not know what it could be. At the same came a noise more terrible than anything he had heard in his whole life. He went forward to ask Karl what was happening.

"It's the zoo. Those poor animals do not know what is going on and are terrified. They are trapped in their cages and so cannot run away as they would in the wild. I am sorry. The only advice I can offer is to grit your teeth and run past as quickly as you can."

In due course Hans followed this advice and eventually fell in an exhausted, traumatised heap on the ground. As he lay there he thought not only about the animals but also about the person who had been not only their friend but his also, Olga Muller. He took the now crumpled self -portrait from his breast pocket and studied it yet again. Never had he met another girl he would consider marrying. Only one came anywhere near to her and that was very different. Remembrance of his sister brought him back to his feet ready for the onward journey.

At last amongst the ruins, he found what remained of the Mothers and babies home. There he saw a blood-stained mother, who might be Frieda, nursing a blood-stained baby. He heard her mutter

"They have killed my Sophia before she could be baptised. She will not be able to get into heaven."

Hans cradled his dead niece in his arms and sang her a lullaby. However he had no words of comfort for his sister. When the matron turned up, he was ashamed to feel relief. Then he told them, truthfully, that he was worried about getting back to camp in time and made his escape, swearing revenge on the bloody English murderers.

A Child of Cologne

24

Visitors

By the summer of 1942 the dry rot was under control and many of the repairs to the hall had been completed. There was always work to do on the farm, especially now the harvest was looming. Nevertheless, at Friday meetings, various people voiced the thought that there was more to life than work and began to suggest activities to fill the long winter evenings that were to come. James' idea of putting on another panto was welcomed. He suggested Snow White and the Seven Dwarves but did not want to give members of the community the Disney names. The new list consisted of Marey, Milky, Ramsey, Curly, Nanny, Cocky and Gandy. No sooner had he read out his suggestions than objections were raised. Reginald objected to Ramsey.

"I am a life-long supporter of the Labour Party and Ramsay MacDonald betrayed us."

The next objection was from Frank and on quite different grounds.

"We, of all people, should not be making fun of the Indian leader who is upholding the ideal of passive resistance for all to follow."

The final objection came from Margaret who said, "We have only acquired the goat very recently but I for one hope it will be gone well before the pantomime season. I cannot afford to have any more of my washing devoured straight off the line."

The other mothers provided a chorus of agreement.

With relief James told the meeting that he would reduce the number from seven to four. What he did not say was that this meant he had fewer parts to write.

Other proposals included a concert featuring both residents and village talent; poetry readings and also speakers.

William said, "What about J.B. Priestley? I used to love listening to his broadcasts until the government made the BBC ban him for being 'too political'. I'd like to learn what some of his plays really mean – from the horse's mouth, so to speak." There was a clamour of agreement.

It was also suggested that if they invited Priestly they should also invite Richard Acland. Everyone knew who he was but some were more hesitant to invite an MP who would be unpopular with the villagers.

"We don't want talks from two leaders of the Common Wealth Party close together."

"No! But I hear Priestley's leaving because he won't accept Acland as leader."

"I'd love to hear J.B. speak," James said. "It was always such a pleasure to listen to his voice and he is so full of wisdom. On the other hand, Common Wealth is the movement of the future for this country. We ought to find out what its leader is like and what he has to say."

Karl intervened to say: "Richard Acland's the MP for the area of Devon around Buckfastleigh. He's not very popular with his constituents since he resigned the Liberal Party Whip to found the Common Wealth movement, but I think he's a remarkable man. He's trying to align his politics with the teachings of Jesus and he and his family have given thousands of acres to the National Trust, the largest donation ever. And he's written a book of prayers for his fellow Anglicans."

The community decided to ask Richard Acland to speak one evening in September and J.B. Priestley in November. The villagers were to be invited to both talks, as well as to most of the other events being planned.

In the end, the only outsiders who turned up to hear the first speaker were the head of the village school, the local GP and a Methodist local preacher. Acland made an impassioned, stirring speech about right and wrong but his audience did not warm to him.

The Queen Anne room was full to bursting for J. B. Priestley's talk and the questions addressed to him afterwards made clear that his rural audience was far more interested in his plays than in his politics.

Richard Stokes also came to give a talk. The Labour MP for Rowell was an outspoken critic of the indiscriminate bombing of Germany. During his speech, he referred to a recently published Gallup poll which showed that, although most people approved of the bombing of German civilians, only half those living in London and other heavily bombed areas did so. Members of the community listened to him with sympathy, but visiting villagers booed.

Other visitors had a more practical focus. The arrival of a team from the War Agricultural Executive Committee was viewed with trepidation by the Southolt community but, in fact, they were far more interested in giving useful advice than in being hypercritical. Teachers from the village school brought their children to see the lambs, piglets and chicks from time to time.

Rowell Quakers held a meeting for worship at the hall and gave a talk on Quakerism. However, much to William and Betty's disappointment, this particular attempt at outreach fell on deaf ears.

Over time the Southolt community became more accepted by the villagers. On harvest Sunday, the community gave some of its produce to the church. Several of the members joined in the annual pram race. The race had only one rule: the members of each team had to drink a pint at all seven pubs in the village. The hall team failed to finish. However, the straw-filled French nun trying to escape over the convent wall won first prize in the scarecrow competition that also formed part of the harvest celebrations. Olga did not approve but found herself laughing nevertheless.

***

Sam used his third weekly letter to berate William. "Once my back was turned you handed my home over to a rabble of conchies, bolshies and scroungers," he wrote.

Olga was going to tea with Lady Stubbs the next day, so she made a copy of the letter to take with her. Sam could only have got his information from her.

"Why couldn't you have given William a chance to explain before upsetting both Sam and William like this? William has only been trying to do what's in Sam's best interests. Would you want Sam to come back and find his home in ruins?"

Amelia broke in as soon as Olga paused for breath. "Yes, I would, actually. Because then he'd have to come and live at Stubbs Hall with me." Amelia realised that she had said more in the heat of the moment than she had intended. She would need to build bridges if she was not to lose everything now Olga's eyes had been opened. Should Sam ever get to hear what she had just said it would be the end of their friendship, let alone anything more. She quickly pulled the rope to summon the butler and afternoon tea.

While they took tea, they worked together on a letter to Sam which explained the situation in a much kinder way.

After tea Amelia suggested that she should add a paragraph to the letter giving news of the horses. Halfway through, she stopped writing "Oh! I'm sorry I forgot you were going for a ride on Magic. Do you still want it?"

Olga was glad Amelia had mentioned it first: she had not known how to remind her discreetly.

Amelia brought the lovely black mare out of the stables and watched while Olga rode her round the field at a walking pace. The girl had good control, she thought. Olga urged Magic into a trot just as a hare chose to make a dash into the open. Magic reared, Olga lost her grip and fell onto the hard path.

She felt Amelia gently probing her body to find out what damage had been done. She could hear questions being asked but could not reply. Then she felt strong arms lifting her up and carrying her inside and upstairs.

When Olga came to, she was full of morphine in a bed in Rowell general hospital and the morning light told her it was the next day.

And this next day was her twenty-first birthday.

Her first visitors were Betty and William. They brought a present of a pair of jodhpurs as well as a birthday cake. They did little more than wish her a happy birthday and give her a kiss before departing, thinking an overlong visit might tire her too much. The hospital staff quickly came in and squirrelled the cake away.

A group of inmates from the hall came with loads of cards, many homemade, and another birthday cake. The hospital staff swooped again.

Finally came Amelia. She had not known it was Olga's birthday but had brought a dozen yellow roses and a Victoria sponge, which also disappeared.

Olga noticed that Amelia also brought with her the unmistakable aroma of 4711 eau de Cologne. And she looked different. She had had a perm, and was wearing make-up that had been applied with expertise. Olga realised that her face now appeared be … interesting. She said so, managing to keep the surprise out of her voice, and asked if she might draw her visitor's portrait.

"Thank you so much! That's the nicest thing anyone has ever said to me in my whole life." She sat down beside the bed, held Olga's hand and said, "It was my idea that you went for a ride so I feel responsible for your getting injured and I am so sorry. Please forgive me."

Olga told her not to talk rubbish and thanked her for taking such good care of her after the fall. "The nurses say that my injuries would have been much worse had it not been for you," she said, squeezing Amelia's hand.

They remained hand in hand, talking until the end of visiting hours. Before she left, Amelia leaned over and kissed Olga on the forehead.

Olga resumed her weekly visits to Stubbs Hall as soon as she left hospital. At first she refused to ride again but Amelia insisted and, at last, Olga succumbed.

***

The Rowans rarely went to the cinema because most films were full of violence or other kinds of immorality. Olga would have liked to go more often but public transport was infrequent and she was reluctant to bother her busy hosts. However, when she saw in the local paper that the Odeon in Rowell was to show a film she particularly wanted to see, she plucked up her courage.

"*Bambi*'s on next week and I very much want to see it. Please could you take me into Rowell when you're going to meeting on Sunday morning, please? I can make my own way back."

William replied at once, giving Betty no chance to speak. "No, my dear. I don't approve of cinemas opening on Sunday and don't want to encourage the practice. There are six other days in the week on which people can go to the cinema. In any case, what about mass?"

"I was trying to fit in. It can't matter if I miss mass once in a blue moon."

"We have to be at the monthly business meeting in Rowell meeting house next Wednesday afternoon. Why don't we take you to the cinema on the way and then you can find us there afterwards? We'll be finished about half past four, with any luck."

"Oh! That would be very kind. But Wednesday is my day for visiting Amelia and she'll expect me mid-afternoon."

"I'm sure that if you send her a note she'll understand."

And so that is what happened.

The business meeting ran very late and the Rowans came out to find Olga in floods of tears. They could not understand what had upset her but managed to make out that, in the film, someone's mother had been killed. On the way back, Betty and William were too busy fiercely continuing their discussion of the real life problem that had already taken up so much of the afternoon that they could not spare time to consider a fictional one. So, Olga's distress was compounded by the rare sight of her two friends at loggerheads and they exchanged perfunctory farewells at Stubbs Hall.

Olga rang the bell.

Amelia answered the door herself. "How dare you treat me like this?" she said. "Who do you think you are?" More questions came thick and fast, and it was obvious Amelia was feeling neglected. "You pretend to be my friend but you've revealed your true colours today. *Bambi*'s a sentimental piece of Marxist rubbish. You've lived in a city all your life and don't know what the real world's like. If no one hunted, the country would be

271

overrun with deer and most of the trees would be destroyed. Even your communist friend, Sir Richard Acland, has enough common sense to allow stag hunting on his vast estates."

Olga pulled herself up from underneath the withering arrows of scorn. "*Bambi*'s mother was killed by evil men of violence and so was mine," she retorted. And, with that, she turned on her heel and walked back home.

Early the next morning, Betty shouted up to Olga that she had a visitor. Amelia stood at the door with a dozen yellow roses in her hands and tears in her eyes.

The two women hugged and forgave each other while agreeing to disagree.

25

Jordans

By early 1944, the work Olga could find to do at the hall was no longer enough to keep her fully occupied. William found her a job with John Nathan, a Quaker solicitor in Rowell whose secretary had just left to get married. John soon realised that Olga was hardworking and intelligent and the work she had earlier done for William proved useful. Olga did not find the job enthralling but John was a good employer and, for the first time, she felt independent. The bus ride of an hour each way was tedious at first, but she soon came to enjoy using it for a combination of looking at the Suffolk countryside and reading.

She continued to receive a letter from Sam each month but they said little except that he was bored, bored and bored. He would always make some reference to the pictures she had drawn for him and how much she reminded him of Helen. Amelia also got monthly letters from him and the two women would worry over him when they met. One day, Amelia remembered Sam saying that he might have a go at becoming a chartered accountant – if he could ever find time to study. Olga responded by saying that he would have plenty of time now.

The next day, Amelia bought a first-class ticket and caught an early train from Manningtree to London. She then took a taxi to Chartered Accountants' Hall and demanded to see the man in charge. When she explained what she wanted, the official told her that it would be normal for a prisoner of war to ask for permission to study for their exams themselves. Amelia persisted, and he eventually agreed to send the necessary papers to Sam for him to fill in and return.

Sam's next letter to Amelia was full of gratitude for her brilliant idea and the effort she had put in. When she replied, she resisted the temptation to take all the praise for herself and told him that the initial idea had been Olga's. As she did so, she could not help whispering aloud, "Fool!" Olga might have become her friend but, at the end of the day, she remained a rival.

Sam's other two letters each month were sent to William and dealt with mundane matters. His earlier anger had evaporated: he knew that he could not unscramble an omelette, however much he wished to. William welcomed his decision to study because it would potentially benefit the management of the estate as well as being good for Sam himself.

On 6 June, the Allies re-entered Western Europe. Churchill had described El Alamein as "the end of the beginning" and the invasion might have been described as "the beginning of the end" because the Red Army was already moving relentlessly forward and Germany's final defeat could no longer be in doubt. But when, how and what would happen afterwards were still wide-open questions.

Talks and concerts resumed in the Autumn but generated less interest. Many members of the community were worrying about what would happen to them when the war was over. The major would return and they would all have to leave the sanctuary of the hall. Jobs would be offered to those presumed to be heroes rather than those presumed to be cowards. But there was little they could do except wait and pray.

On Christmas Eve, Betty received a mysterious phone call from Stella, asking her to visit and to make sure to bring Olga. She would not be drawn further over the phone. To his surprise and disappointment William had not been invited, not that he could have gone anyway because he was in charge of cooking the home-raised geese that were, as usual, to be the central part of the Christmas dinner. Olga was disappointed to be missing Christmas morning mass but was curious to find out why Stella wanted her there. Betty knew that there would be a programmed meeting for worship on Christmas Day and thought that attending a programmed Quaker meeting might challenge Olga's conscience. She therefore gave Olga her present – a copy of *A Christmas Carol* – early, suggesting that she could read in another room while the meeting was being held.

Betty and Olga set off early on Christmas morning, aiming to reach Jordans by half past ten when the annual programmed meeting for worship, which would include carols and special Christmas readings and carols. Olga was nominally navigator but she had never read a map before so was of little help. Betty did not remember the route as well as she had hoped and the roads were still not signposted, although the danger of invasion had passed. She took several wrong turns and the flurries of snow were getting more frequent. Twice she stopped the car to ask pedestrians where they were. On the second occasion the passer-by told her that they were entering Warwick. Betty relayed this information to Olga adding

"We must be quite near to Stratford and that has reminded that, on the very first day we met I promised to take you there. I'd forgotten till now. Please forgive me."

"Of course. We have been a little preoccupied since then! And I've so much to be thankful for. If it was possible I would particularly like to see a performance of Romeo and Juliet."

The snow turned into a blizzard while Olga proudly displayed her knowledge of Warwick the Kingmaker and his part in the Wars of the Roses. Betty was impressed but wished her companion knew as much about the geography of England as she did about history. Soon they were entering another place but this time they recognised its identity without asking. Only Coventry in this part of the country could have had so many bombed buildings. Betty drove slowly past them until they stopped beside the ruins of the cathedral.

Since entering the bombed area Olga had been quiet. She was visualising what the ruins in that other city, the one she knew and loved so much, would be looking like. Words were rushing round and round in her head until the car had stopped and she had seen what remained of the ancient shrine. The words exploded: "A plague on both your houses!"

No sooner than the words had come out then a wave of remorse filled Olga and, after collecting herself somewhat, she said, "That is most unfair. The Nazis murdered my mother and my grandmother and countless other innocent people. The men in the RAF are risking their lives in the hope that their actions might shorten the War. I feel so ashamed for being so ungrateful."

Betty put her arms around her German friend and said, "Look. A cross of charred timbers has been erected as a symbol that a new cathedral will arise at this place after the war is over."

They did not reach Jordans till the meeting for worship was over and the Quakers had gathered in the schoolroom for coffee and mince pies. She could not believe her eyes because, amongst those gathered was an army officer in British uniform and a group of men wearing a strange uniform. Stella came to greet the new arrivals. She started to introduce them to the assembled company but was interrupted.

"I don't want to meet any more of you damned English murderers!" cried someone, in German. "You killed my little Sophia."

Olga froze. The man shouting sounded like Hans. Surely it could not be him? Or was it somehow possible? What he was saying made no sense. Her grandmother had been murdered by Nazis not the English. In any case she had been tall, everyone knew that, no one could have described her as 'little.' Then she saw the person who had shouted and horrified, realised that it *was* Hans. He was barely recognisable, his face was so badly disfigured and it was clear he was blind. She went up to him and quietly said his name.

He jumped. "Go away!" he shouted. "I know you! You're a figment of my imagination. You're not real. Stop haunting me!"

Stella intervened, also speaking in German. "Hans, you're spoiling the party for all the other prisoners. Please, come with me." She called Robert over, beckoned Betty and Olga to follow and, between them, they bundled Hans out of the classroom, into the car park and into the back seat of their car. Stella asked Betty and Olga to sit on either side of him. Olga tried to hold his hand but her one-time close friend failed to respond.

Stella tried to calm Hans and explain her plan "Don't worry Hans we are going to take you to our house. You might be happier with fewer people around." We will bring you back later on."

Robert drove, with Stella beside him. After a short distance Robert signalled that he was turning right. Before they turned Stella said to Olga

"This road continues to Slough."

Olga responded "Is Slough the place that John Betjeman is talking about in his poem?"

Stella admitted that it was but also said that she thought he had been most unfair.

When they got to Oasis Cottage, they led Hans out of the car and into the lounge. He had stopped shouting but looked completely confused. Stella offered him a cup of tea which he grudgingly accepted saying he hoped it was not poisoned. Stella reassured him truthfully, but did not admit that she had dropped in a sedative. Once he was asleep, they carried him upstairs to the spare bed.

Stella was expecting some friends, a family of Jewish refugees from Vienna, in an hour's time. She had got to know Mary and Joseph at events organised by Young Austria, a group set up by Slough Quakers with help from Jordans. They were coming round today to celebrate their daughter Eve's sixth birthday and Stella was concerned about Eve being in the house at the same time as Hans in his present state of mind. However, it was too late to contact them and ask them not to come. Robert reassured the women that it was perfectly safe: Hans would not be able to move around the bedroom, let alone come downstairs, without help. All the same, Stella felt obliged to explain the situation to Mary and Joseph when they arrived. Eve heard too.

The family had been there for about an hour when shouting erupted upstairs. The adults sat for a few moments, uncertain what to do for the best. But Eve shot out of her seat and rushed upstairs. The adults followed as quickly as they could and saw her standing before Hans looking directly into his sightless eyes.

"Hans, please be quiet," Eve said, in German.

Hans fell silent and asked to come downstairs.

Eve settled down to enjoy her presents. Hans wished her a happy birthday and remained quiet throughout the birthday tea and until the family left.

Hans had to be at the POW camp – Wilton Park on the outskirts of Beaconsfield – by seven. Robert drove him back, and Stella went too in order to help Hans from the car to the barracks.

"Well, that was clearly a miracle," said Robert as he took his coat off back at Oasis Cottage.

"You and your miracles!" said Stella smiling. "Hans still can't see, so where's the miracle?"

"His mind is obviously still troubled too," said Betty. "Nevertheless, what Eve did was remarkable."

Olga sat in silence. Her mind was in turmoil as she tried to absorb the events of the past few hours. More than anything else, she wanted to free her friend from his demons and help him with the physical problem of his blindness. But she did not know how.

Stella interrupted her thoughts. "I think we should have an early night. We have had a physically and emotionally wearing day. You two must be exhausted." She said looking at Olga and Betty. "We have been invited to meet the commander of Wilton Park tomorrow. I assume that you will want to come?"

***

Colonel Edwards was a tall, upright man with a military moustache. He greeted his visitors warmly and arranged for tea.

"I've invited you here first of all so I can ask Mr and Mrs Fell to convey my thanks to the Quaker meeting for making my prisoners so welcome yesterday. I think they really appreciated your hospitality, and it was good for them to meet real English people and see someone other than their captors."

283

"I'm not sure that everyone in Britain would regard us as 'real English people'."

"I know what you mean! But I had to start somewhere and the Quakers seemed to be the best place. Spending time with non-combatants is an important step in our de-Nazification and rehabilitation programme. We classify the prisoners as white, black or grey depending on whether they're anti-Nazi, pro-Nazi or somewhere in between. Everyone in the group who came yesterday was white – except for Hans Smit who can't even be properly described as grey. As you may have guessed, it's mainly because of him that I've invited you here."

The colonel said that they were making plans to send the prisoners back to Germany when the war in Europe was over. "None of it is simple but Hans is one of our biggest problems because of his blindness and his mental state. We can't send him out into the jungle that Germany will shortly become alone, and he would be unhappy in a home for the blind in England. I gather that you used to know him, Miss Muller? Can you make any suggestions?"

"Well, I suppose he could stay with me at the hall, but it wasn't really designed for blind people. We expect the owner to be back soon after the war is over, so it would be a temporary solution at best."

Olga saw the puzzled look on the colonel's face and gave a potted history of the Southolt Commonwealth. She sensed that he did not approve but had decided not to say so.

The room fell silent for a while.

"I could marry Hans and go back to Germany with him."

The room was silent no longer.

"You must not throw your life away!"

"That's the most stupid and reckless idea I've ever heard! You no longer know him. He's not only blind, he's disturbed as well."

"How would the pair of you survive in the ruins that so much of Germany is becoming?"

The more they argued, the more Olga felt her own words had trapped her. She held up her hands to ask for peace from their well-meant onslaught.

"I know I can't manage such a difficult task alone. First, I want to go to Germany to find Frieda, if she's still alive, and ask for her help."

The commandant looked at his watch and announced that he had another meeting. He suggested that they meet again to continue the discussions two days later.

Betty went home but Olga stayed with Stella. She was happy to eventually come back by train, having been reassured that the map of the London Underground was much easier to read than the RAC road atlas.

When they met the colonel again, he told them that he had been making inquiries. The powers-that-be had told him it would be better for Olga to travel sooner rather than later because once the war was over Europe would be awash with people looking for their friends and relatives.

"That's the good news," he said. "The bad news is that they won't allow you to travel alone."

"I could go with her," Stella said. "The Friends War Victims Relief Service want someone to go on an exploratory visit and I'd been thinking of offering my services."

"I don't think they would consider your company sufficient. What they're really worried about is women going around unchaperoned while the war's still on."

"I'm working in the HQ of the Friends Ambulance Unit, and we could do with finding out more about the situation in

Germany, so I could go with them." said Robert.

"I don't have the final say but thank you, I think that may do. I'll get in touch with you again when things are more settled."

A Child of Cologne

26

Cologne Again

On Sunday, Stella drove Olga to Slough and put her on a train to Paddington. On the train, Olga read the Sunday newspaper she had bought in the Royal Hotel, catching up with some of the news she had missed during her stay at Oasis Cottage. In an article praising the successful exploits of the RAF she was horrified to discover that Cologne had suffered a recent raid that involved not a thousand bombers, but two thousand. She felt weary and sad when she thought of how often her city – and the catalogue of other cities- which were mentioned in the article, had been bombed time after time. It was impossible to imagine how many had died and what the devastation would be like. Would she recognise Cologne?

Olga reached Liverpool Street station with time to spare but she felt dizzy. She sat on a bench and tried to recall her arrival six years before. For a moment, the dizziness cleared and she had a vision of a statue of children carrying cases and marching purposefully across the station. She came to thinking that it was a lovely idea, even if it would never become reality.

***

Olga had kept up an infrequent but steady exchange of letters with Father Josef after he had written to tell her about the death of her father. She decided that her best hope of finding Frieda was to write to him about her plans.

> *Dear Father Josef,*
>
> *Thank you so much for your Christmas card. It was very special not just because it showed the tomb of the three kings – one of my favourite parts of the cathedral – but also because you had drawn it yourself and the greetings are written in your beautiful Germanic script.*
>
> *A few days ago, I had a very strange experience which I need to tell you about. You probably remember that I used to*

meet Hans Smit, my next-door neighbour, in the cathedral. His parents did not approve of him mixing with a non-Aryan and, in the end, we had to stop meeting.

At the time of Kristallnacht, he smuggled a message to me saying that my life was in danger and I needed to escape. I received it just before I found the body of your sister-in-law, my dear grandmother. I heard nothing about him after that.

But then I met him again on Christmas Day! He was at a party the Quakers were holding for POWs. He had become a pilot and had crashed his plane in England. The accident has left him blind and his face is badly scarred. What is possibly worse is that he is mentally disturbed. During the party he was shouting (in German, fortunately), "You damned English murderers killed my little Sophia." Such a statement will, presumably, make as little sense to you as it does to me but illustrates how far his mind has wandered from reality.

The commander of the camp is most concerned about what will happen to Hans when the time comes to repatriate

*the prisoners. In the heat of the moment,
I said that I'd marry Hans and take him
back to Germany with me. As an
afterthought, I added that I planned to
try and find his sister, Frieda, first in the
hope that she might help me.*

*I know that what I'm proposing to do
is crazy but I've committed myself and I
can see no alternative. It is said that
every quest starts with the first step, but
I've little idea what my first step should
be. Can you offer me any advice, please,
from your wealth of experience?*

Your ever-loving grandniece,
Olga

***

The next month seemed to go on forever.
Saint Valentine's Day was usually a day of
silly fun, but not this year. Olga sensed a
mood of sombre reflection in the village. She
was sad to hear about the bombing of
Dresden but she did not think it much more
beautiful or historic than many other targets.
So it was very confusing to find that people
who rarely spoke to her were coming up to
apologise. These same people had said
previously that other German cities were

simply getting a taste of their own medicine when the bombs fell on them. When someone described the British government as a bull in a china shop, the penny dropped. To kill people as part of the war effort was forgivable but to destroy delicate figurines was barbaric.

With the first day of March came early signs of spring. Buttercups and daisies, dandelions and primroses in the fields, the buds beginning to swell on the trees, and birdsong everywhere. After breakfast, Olga went to her favourite seat, the bench just outside the farm which overlooked the vale. She started sketching the ever-changing bank of stratus clouds and the view below. On her left was the footpath which led down to the river. Sometimes, in the summer, members of the community would go down the path and enjoy a picnic on the banks of the Stour. On a couple of occasions they had ventured further, going across the bridge to Dedham where they had stopped for afternoon tea at The Essex Rose before returning to their Suffolk village. Of course, on their return, they would not admit to anyone that they had fraternised with folk from the wrong side of the river.

William joined her mid-morning, bringing a flask of tea. "Have you ever heard of Luke Howard?"

"No. Who was he?"

"He was a Quaker scientist who first classified clouds and a great letter writer. He used to write to the artist who loved to paint clouds while sitting in this spot. He also corresponded with your poet, Goethe, who wrote a poem in his honour. However, his most important letters were the ones he wrote persuading the British government to send famine relief to the people of Europe at the end of the Napoleonic Wars."

It was getting colder and the clouds looked more threatening, so they returned to the warmth and comfort of the hall.

***

Three weeks later, Olga received the long-awaited reply from Father Josef.

My dear Olga,

Many thanks for your letter. Yes! I remember you meeting Hans at the cathedral but that is not all I remember about him.

There was a particularly bad air raid in May or June 1942 which we still talk about despite all the others we have suffered. I was giving what comfort I could at the mothers and babies home. It had been destroyed and there were so many mothers who were grieving. I saw Hans carrying a blood-stained baby in his arms and heard him crooning to it although it was clearly dead. I introduced myself to him and he introduced me to the baby's mother who turned out to be Frieda, his sister. In answer to my unspoken question she told me that she did not know who the father was because she had been raped by two German soldiers, both of whom were named Herman. She then said that she had called the baby Sophia, after your grandmother.

Hans went back to his unit and, I'm sorry to say, I don't know what happened to Frieda afterwards. I'll try to find out but can offer little hope.

One bit of good news is that the Americans are now in charge here and are planning to bring Herr Adenauer back to help them.

With lots of love,

A Child of Cologne

Your great-uncle,
Father Josef

And then, three weeks later, there was more from Father Josef. He said that, after sending the previous letter, he had remembered that Father Mathias had been chaplain to the home and so he had asked him what he knew about Frieda's whereabouts. Father Josef had been surprised to discover that Father Mathias had taken Frieda to Rhöndorf and found her a home there with friends of his. So he and Father Mathias had gone to visit Frieda and bring her up to date. They had also visited someone else who was then living in Rhöndorf; Konrad Adenauer. When the ex-mayor had heard the whole story, he said he would be willing to interview Olga for a post in his office. He thought that her recent experience would be useful and, if she was half as good a worker as her father, she would be a Godsend in dealing with the Americans.

Colonel Edwards had been unable to make arrangements for Olga to go to Germany, but Herr Adenauer managed to pull the right strings. Before the end of April after a successful interview with him and a joyful reunion with Frieda. The two friends travelled back to England with the purpose of collecting Hans and taking him back to Cologne and a new life.

Before she left Germany, she made inquiries about the children and staff of the Lawne Jewish School who had been left behind. She was told that they had been herded onto a train, taken to the middle of a forest and massacred. She was also told about the thousand Roma who had been murdered on the steps of the cathedral.

Olga and Frieda had to wait overnight in the Hook of Holland before they could sail to Harwich. They stayed up until the early hours in their hotel discussing the problems that lay ahead. They decided that it was pointless trying to do anything for the moment about the biggest one, finding somewhere to live in the ruins of Cologne, but they did discuss how they could look after Hans on a day-to-day basis.

As they got into bed, Olga said, "There's something I've been wanting to ask you all evening but I've avoided coming out with it. I know you've agreed to help me persuade your brother to be my husband, but will you be my wife? What I mean is, will you let me provide for you and take care of you?"

Frieda put her arms around her and said, "Thank you, dear. And yes, please. After the Hermans raped me I swore an oath that I'd never be any man's wife. This, however, is a very different matter. I will look after Hans and our home during the day while you go off to work. Then you can care for your husband through the night."

27

Peace

In the spring of 1945 there was a bye-election in the neighbouring constituency of Chelmsford. People from the community went to support the Commonwealth candidate. They rejoiced when they helped the movement secure its latest victory. However it was the last one. In the July General Election it lost all the seats, except Chelmsford, and was absorbed by the Labour Party soon afterwards. Subsequently Richard Acland was elected as a Labour MP but resigned over the issue of the Hydrogen bomb.

It was VE Day and the hall, the church and the village were decorated with bunting that people had managed to improvise despite the wartime scarcities. The church bells rang for the first time in almost five years. The hall's solitary bell resumed its pre-war duty of summoning residents for meals and meetings. There were numerous parties in Southolt, but the commonwealth hosted the largest. Many people came but many others boycotted it, still wanting nothing to do with 'the conchies'. This was particularly true of those who had family serving in the Far East or, even worse, had loved ones in Japanese POW camps. Throughout the war, the residents of the hall had seen the attitude of the villagers towards them vary. Things were much worse just after someone in the village had received one of the dreaded War Office telegrams. They chose to avoid visiting any of the pubs at such times, knowing that the insults would escalate and they would be spat at, challenged to fights and called cowards when they refused to respond. The worst culprits were those who had dishonestly shirked active service and felt guilty about it.

28

A New Day Dawns

William and Betty took Olga and Frieda to collect Hans from Wilton Park and say goodbye to Stella, Robert and the Friends at Jordans. After Hans had been collected William drove his passengers to the nearby cottage where the blind Milton had lived during the plague. They all sat in the sunlit garden while Olga described the scene for Hans and he drank in the heady perfume coming from the fruit trees. After a while Hans drifted off to sleep while the others sat in quiet contemplation. He woke with a start and said, in German, I have just composed a poem in my dreams. Can someone write it down for me, please? Frieda took a pad and pen out of her handbag and commenced to record the poem. It was to prove to be the first of many over the rest of his lifetime.

Hans asked if they might stop off in Slough on the way back so he could see Mary, Joseph and Eve before he left. The others were somewhat surprised but were happy to agree.

When they got to the humble home, Hans raised his cap to the little girl. "Thank you so much, Eve. The command you gave to the demon within me on Christmas Day has transformed my life. I doubt if I'll ever be completely cured, but I'm a different man now because of you. Thank you! Thank you!"

Eve went up to Hans and whispered something in his ear but he never told anyone, not even Olga or Frieda, what she had said.

They had anticipated that Hans would face some practical problems at the hall, but most were far from insurmountable. The biggest problem was altogether unexpected – the first time he smelt and heard the farm animals, Hans started screaming. Olga cradled him in her arms to comfort him and try and find out what was troubling him. Once he had explained, it was his turn to comfort her.

"My poor, poor friends," she sobbed, thinking of all the animals and humans she had known. she sobbed. They cried in each other's arms until they were exhausted.

Hans gradually came to terms with the farm but he never became a real animal lover. He obstinately refused to countenance the idea of marriage for a long time but, in the end, he was no match for the two women in his life.

***

On the morning of the big day, Frieda was looking after Hans in his room and Olga was sitting quietly in her room when she heard a knock on her door. She opened it. Sam strode in and slammed the door shut behind him.

"I'm sorry I've left this so late, but I've only just arrived and found out what you're planning to do. You must not do this. To give your beauty to a man who can't see you is wanton waste. I won't allow it!"

Olga could smell that he had been drinking. "Please go away and don't spoil my day," she said. "I love Hans and I *am* going to marry him, whatever you say."

It seemed that Sam sensed defeat but was unwilling to give up without a fight. He saw the diamond earrings on her dressing table.

"At least promise to wear those today – and on special occasions in the future. Then

I'll have the consolation of knowing that you're thinking of me sometimes."

Olga snatched them up from and thrust them into his hands. "Please, give these to Amelia as soon as possible. Ask her to marry you. She loves you very much and, in a marriage, love is far more important than loveliness."

Sam had not visited Amelia since he had come back. His relationship with her was all right while he remained at a distance but he knew he would be embarrassed to see her again in the flesh. There was too much of it.

Sam sat in a secluded part of Saint Edward's for the ceremony, staring at the back of Olga's head and imagining how the earrings would have looked on her petite ears. He joined everyone else in the Queen Anne room for the wedding breakfast, which was modest as rationing was still very much in force. When the eating and the toasts were over James Green got out his guitar and played *The Blue Danube*. With difficulty Hans led his bride in the first, formal steps of the dance. He then, gratefully and gracefully gave way to those less handicapped than himself,

Again Sam had stationed himself in a secluded spot where he could view the other people present. He decided he would not stay for long after the dancing began. But then he noticed an attractive woman on the other side of the room. The army had taken away a little of his shyness but he was still nervous in situations like this. His inner voice kept nudging him. *If you don't act now you may never see her again.* So, eventually, he got up and crossed the room.

"Good evening. My name is Sam Browne and …"

Amelia's bright smile and amused, quiet laugh opened his eyes. Before he could say more, she took his hand and led him outside where the normally shy couple walked and talked until they heard the strains of *The Last Waltz* being played. Early the next morning Sam appeared at Stubbs Hall with the earrings and his proposal

***

The Smits agreed to spend their short honeymoon in Southolt so Frieda and Hans could experience some of what Olga had felt for the home she was about to leave. So, after lunch, Olga led Hans and Frieda to the bench at the edge of the farm and, for the benefit of her husband she described the view of the vale in front of them. She then went on to say, "On the eve of the war, Betty and William took me to London. We saw many things and visited many places but the most important to me were the art galleries. I loved looking at the work of so many famous names but, time after time, I wished that Daddy was with me. The paintings I most wanted to see were those by the artist who was born up the road from this spot. I wanted to see how they compared to the real thing, this view. I wasn't disappointed, they gave me a deeper understanding and appreciation. I was particularly lucky to see the ones in the National Gallery because they have been moved to a vault deep inside a Welsh mountain for the duration."

"The cathedral's glass was taken away and stored too," said Frieda. "People are saying that the spaces left behind are were what prevented it from collapsing during the bombing."

After that the trio sat with their separate reveries of the previous day's events. In particular Olga recalled that after the dance

Frieda had gently helped her take off the precious wedding dress. Olga had hugged her and said, "Thank you so much for everything, my dear. Today God has, I believe, not only joined me to Hans but also to you."

Frieda had agreed and added, "But the Church will never see it like that. However, I think God understands and there is, therefore, no need for us to confess our love to a priest."

The girls had kissed each other before Olga had joined Hans in the nuptial bed.

***

The Smits received a message from Herr Adenauer to say that the British Military had replaced the Americans in Cologne and that they did not want him anymore. He was going back to Rhöndorf and he would be very pleased to welcome them there. Frieda said that they should have little trouble in finding a home in the village.

William and Betty drove the trio to Harwich to set off for their new life in Germany. "Please come back and have a holiday with us soon. I'll then have the opportunity to fulfil my promise to take Olga to visit Stratford."

"Thank you. I'd love that."

It was not long before Olga came back for the wedding of her friends, Amelia and Sam. During the visit Betty managed to organise a trip to Stratford where the Shakespeare Memorial Theatre happened to be putting on a performance of Romeo and Juliet.

Once they were settled, Olga searched for the rest of her family. She discovered that Ursula had been sent away from the Gestapo headquarters to a concentration camp but she never found out which one. This was hard news for Olga to take to her other grandmother who was living alone in Bonn. She had been widowed and both Otto and Marguerite had abandoned her.

Hans and Olga's baby daughter was born in a pretty cottage on the banks of the Rhine. Of course, they named her Sophia. She gave a new lease of life to Frau Nachtigall who was delighted to be a great-grandmother. In time, they had two sons, naming the elder Siegfried and the younger Heinrich. Frieda was godmother to all three.

***

A Child of Cologne

In late 1948, Olga received an invitation to the re-opening of the cathedral. It was now deemed safe to use. She arrived early and knelt for a long time in front of the Gero Cross. Out of the vast silence she experienced a voice. Afterwards she did not know whether it was the voice of God the Father or of her father, Heinrich, or a co-mingling of them both. What she did know was what it had said:

~ Welcome Home, Child of Cologne
~

Made in the USA
Coppell, TX
08 August 2021